On Wings of Silence

On Wings of Silence:
Mexico '68

Dede Fox

LITERARY PRESS
LAMAR UNIVERSITY

ISBN: 978-1-942956-67-9
Library of Congress Control Number: 2019936225

Manufactured in the United States

Lamar University Literary Press
Beaumont, Texas

For all the Guillermos and Guillerminas

Recent Poetry from Lamar University Literary Press

Bobby Aldridge, *An Affair of the Stilled Heart*
Michael Baldwin, *Lone Star Heart, Poems of a Life in Texas*
Charles Behlen, *Failing Heaven*
Alan Berecka, *With Our Baggage*
David Bowles, *Flower, Song, Dance: Aztec and Mayan Poetry*
Jerry Bradley, *Crownfeathers and Effigies*
Jerry Bradley and Ulf Kirchdorfer, editors, *The Great American Wise Ass Poetry Anthology*
Matthew Brennan, *One Life*
Julie Chappel, *Mad Habits of a Life*
Paul Christensen, *The Jack of Diamonds is a Hard Card to Play*
Christopher Carmona, Rob Johnson, and Chuck Taylor, editors, *The Beatest State in the Union*
Chip Dameron, *Waiting for an Etcher*
William Virgil Davis, *The Bones Poems*
Jeffrey DeLotto, *Voices Writ in Sand*
Chris Ellery, *Elder Tree*
Larry Griffin, *Cedar Plums*
Ken Hada, *Margaritas and Redfish*
Michelle Hartman, *Disenchanted and Disgruntled*
Katherine Hoerth, *Goddess Wears Cowboy Boots*
Lynn Hoggard, *Motherland*
Godspower Oboido, *Wandering Feet on Pebbled Shores*
Gretchen Johnson, *A Trip Through Downer, Minnesota*
Ulf Kirchdorfer, *Chewing Green Leaves*
Laozi, *Daodejing*, tr. By David Breeden, Steven Schroeder, and Wally Swist
Janet McCann, *The Crone at the Casino*
Erin Murphy, *Ancilla*
Laurence Musgrove, *Local Bird*
Dave Oliphant, *The Pilgrimage, Selected Poems: 1962-2012*
Kornelijus Platelis, *Solitary Architectures*
Carol Coffee Reposa, *Underground Musicians*
Jan Seale, *The Parkinson Poems*
Steven Schroeder, *the moon, not the finger, pointing*
Glen Sorestad *Hazards of Eden*
W.K. Stratton, *Ranchero Ford/ Dying in Red Dirt Country*
Loretta Diane Walker, *Desert Light*
Wally Swist, *Invocation*
Jonas Zdanys (ed.), *Pushing the Envelope, Epistolary Poems*
Jonas Zdanys, *Red Stones*
Jonas Zdanys, *Three White Horses*

For information on these and other Lamar University Literary Press books go to
www.Lamar.edu/literarypress

"La vida no es la que uno vivio, sino la que uno recuerda, y como la recuerda para contrarla."

Life is not what one has lived, but rather what one remembers, and how one remembers it to recount it.

Gabriel Garcia Marquez

Other books by Dede Fox

The Treasure in the Tiny Blue Tin

Confessions of a Jewish Texan

Postcards Home

PART I: EXPLORING THE NEW WORLD

"They walked in the *Jardin Independencia* where high above them stood a white stone angel with one broken wing. From her stone wrists dangled the broken chains of the manacles she wore."

Cormac McCarthy
All the Pretty Horses

"There are two breeds of writers: the poet, who hearkens to an inner voice, his own; and the novelist, the journalist and the historian, who hearken to many voices in the world round them, the voices of others."

Octavio Paz
Massacre in Mexico

Pan Am 707: August, 1968

The plane rolls and bucks
over jagged mountains
that rim Mexico City.
We   up.
  fall   rises
   and   earth
     the

"¡*Ay, Dios mio!*"
A silver-haired woman
raises a diamond-heavy hand
and drops her rosary at my feet.

I pick it up,
its brown beads
warm and smooth,
and return it to her.
"*Qué loco paseo,*
like a roller coaster!"
I say, as we ascend again.

"¿Are you going to our Olympics?"
She presses a lace handkerchief
to her forehead and responds
to my nod. "An athlete?"

I laugh. "No. My drama teacher once said
I have the grace of a flea-bitten rabbit."
I blot a greasy splotch of butter
that I dropped on my mini-skirt
before the white-gloved stewardess
picked up my lunch tray
and the *vieja's* brimming ashtray.

Señora folds her hanky
into tiny squares.
"¿*Traveling alone?*"

"Yes."
What I don't say:
I love it.

"But you're so young.
How old are you?"

"Eighteen," I lie.

"A young girl alone in the city?
So dangerous! Be careful."

My stomach bumps against my ribs
as the plane dips to the right,
I frown at her warning,
press my powdered nose
against the layered glass window,
for a glimpse of my new world,
the tree-lined boulevards, museums,
parks I've seen in colored postcards.

Mother and Dad were dead-set against
my attending college in Mexico,
but since I worked part-time jobs
for four long years during high school
and saved every penny
to pay my own way,
they didn't stop me.
I push my fears aside.

This is finally *my* chance to fly.

Cosmic Question

Once I asked Mother,
"Is this all there is?
Am I supposed to:
            go to college,
            meet a husband,
            get married,
            raise children,
and then it starts
all over again
with my daughters?"

With thinning lips,
she said, "What else
would you want?"

I backed away
from the sharp edges
in her voice.

I want more,
much more,
and so did she
or she wouldn't have been
so angry.

Good Girls

...never leave the house
without putting on their faces.
They wear bras, girdles, and slips
under their shirtwaists.

...wear white gloves to tea parties,
eat no more than two finger sandwiches,
and one sweet treat. They do not
clatter forks, burp, or break china.

...have a nine o'clock curfew
on weekdays and twelve o'clock
on weekends because Mother says,
"Nothing good ever happens after midnight."

...don't have sex before marriage.
In my father's words,
"If you give away the milk,
why would anyone want to buy the cow?"

...study hard,
make good grades,
good enough to get into a good college
where they can meet a good husband.

...marry by age 22
and 2 to 4 years later
have 2 to 4 children
with equal numbers of boys and girls.

Mother quotes a neighbor
who went to "finishing" school,
says Mrs. Charles Pearson learned
a woman should never talk about politics,
religion, or sex in mixed company.
Easy for Mrs. Charles Pearson to say.
She's home all day with five snotty kids.
Talk about finished.

Incognito

My family and friends won't see me
until December and will only talk
with me for a few minutes on static-filled
way-too-expensive long-distance calls.
They will only know
                              what I write home
                              how *I say* I am ...

Plotting My Story

Writers slip out of their own
skins into someone else's.
They live many lives.

That's my plan,
to meet lots of people,
travel in exotic places
so I have more to write about,
experiences far from the rundown
strip centers and baked parking lots of Texas
where nothing but bad weather ever happens.

And then there is that secret hope,
buried deep in the shallow pockets
of my yellow mini-skirt.
I don't want to be married,
like my sister Libby,
but I *do* want to find someone
who sees and loves the whole of me,
the Diana Greene, unknown,
even to my family
and me.

"¡Bienvenido a Mexico!"

As I descend the rollaway stairs
from the aircraft to the tarmac,
Melinda, my roommate from Lafayette,
waves her arms like a cheerleader
and runs up to embrace me.

We wrote letters all summer, exchanged
photos, but none captured her energy.
A tiny girl, Melinda has strawberry blonde curls
that bounce every which way
when she moves, and she's always moving.
"Did you survive your sister's wedding?"

I laugh and say, "Barely.
It was two nights ago."

"Well, you're here now,
and southern girls know
how to have us some fun."
She gives me another hug.
"*Chango*, a guy I'm dating,
will drive us to the apartment."

"*Chango?* Monkey?" I ask.

Melinda giggles.
"All the boys here have nicknames.
Chango is hairy like a monkey,
but funny and cute.
I don't know his real name."

"So you like him?"

"Maybe," she says. "There he is!"
She points to a guy with thick eyebrows,
long sideburns, and an easy smile.
He takes my suitcases, make-up case,
and typewriter and packs them into a VW,
leaving just enough room for Melinda
to stretch out on top of the luggage,
her head behind his while I ride shotgun.

My Spanish is choppy and awkward,
his English nonexistent so

I soak up the blue-sky day
and gawk at my new world.

Chango zigzags through traffic,
singing about my roommate,
muy linda, "very cute,"
until, blushing, Melinda reaches over
to tickle the back of his hairy neck.

Then the words change to *mi Linda,*
"my Linda." Windows down, we sing
together until we stop short at a red light,
barely missing a boy who runs up
to my window calling, *"Chicle!"*

I give him a quarter for a small pack
of gum and *Chango* frowns, warns me,
"Si usted compra goma de un mendigo,
pronto tendremos una larga línea
de ellos siguiéndonos."

I understand enough to know
he doesn't approve,
or want children trailing after his car,
but offer *Chango* gum anyway.

Apparently, he doesn't mind chewing
peppermint Chicklets, just buying
packs from raggedy children.

Olympic Flames

The city hurries to put on
its best face for the games.
Students stand on many corners,
handing out leaflets
or holding Che Guevara signs.

A rainbow of Olympic posters,
usually on construction sites,
advertises coming events.
Six weeks away and counting.

The green prints of Aztec calendars
and Olympic rings are perfect souvenirs,

my favorite is a white dove,
La Paloma de Paz.

Chango sees me pointing.
"Es el tema de los juegos.
Todo es posible en la paz."

"Everything is possible in peace,"
I echo. *"Si, entiendo.*
Es verdad." The truth.
Only one hour in Mexico
and already I have a writing topic.
I pull out a small spiral
from my purse, a pencil
from behind my ear,
and take notes.

Chango frowns again.
Apparently, I'm making
a negative impression
and I have no idea why.

Behind me,
an electric typewriter rattles.
Grandma gave it to me
for graduation, the perfect gift.

Now
I can do
and say
and write
                    what I want

without my family
censoring
my every move.

My time is my own,
whether *Chango* likes it
or not.

Outside Señora Salina's Apartment

Chango somehow squeezes the car
into the tiniest of spots along its curb
before he offers Melinda his hand
and pulls her from the back
of the VW into his arms.

I move around them to grab
my typewriter and make-up case.
He breaks away to unload suitcases
before handing a uniformed man
some coins and saying something
to him in a low voice.

"Does this apartment have a bellman?"
I ask Melinda.

"No," she whispers back. "If *Chango* doesn't pay
the guy to 'watch' his car, it may be damaged
or stolen. That's just how it works here."

The sidewalk shakes beneath my feet.
I brace myself against a wall.
My make-up case vibrates too.
"Uh, hello," I say, "is this an earthquake?"

Melinda raises her hand in an I-don't-know gesture.
"There are earthquakes here all the time,
but it could be tunneling for the subway.
It's going in next to the building.
We never know *what's* shaking."

Chango repeats, "What's shaking!" and laughs.
Guess he knows some English after all.

Inside Señora Salina's Apartment

"Sra. Salinas? Esta aqui?" Melinda calls,
dragging in a suitcase twice her size.

"No, but I'm here," answers a curvy girl
with olive skin, brown eyes, and full,
heart-shaped lips.

"Cool," Melinda says.
"So we can talk
without the *señora* listening.
She's kind of nosy."

"Kind of? You're being way too kind."
The curvy girl smiles and says, "I'm Natalie.
Welcome home, such as it is."

Heavy drapes hang over the windows,
giving the place a dusty, dreary look.

Melinda scoots the suitcases under my bed
as the room shakes again, like the whole building
might collapse into a subway tunnel at any minute.

I must look as panicked as I feel
because Melinda says, "Don't freak out.
After we register for classes on Wednesday,
Natalie and I are going to the housing office
to request a transfer to another place.
You can come with us."

"There's got to be a better place
than this," I say, with one hand
against a vibrating wall.

"Definitely."

"Let's get out of here and have some fun,"
says Melinda, definitely the party girl
in our group.

Natalie digs under a bed to get her purse.
"My parents signed me up for a *deportivo,*
like a YMCA. Indoor and outdoor pools.
Great people watching."

We're out the door
to start my new life.

Walking to the *Deportivo*

We carry our bathing suits in bags
               held close to our bodies
and link arms when crowds on city streets
               part enough for us
to walk three across.

A man follows Melinda,
               asks her the time.
                  She isn't wearing a watch.
                  When I turn my arm to look at mine,
                  Natalie hisses, "Don't do that.
                  He doesn't want the time."

Melinda's curls tangle in the breeze.
        She chats with the stranger
               while Natalie's face darkens.

She stops abruptly and turns to the man.
        "*Vete!* Sister Magdalena is in this store.
        You'll be in big trouble if she sees you
        anywhere near us."
Then she grabs us by the arms
and marches us into a store
where we duck behind a postcard display
                  and watch him.

The man waits, but turns when he sees
the next pretty girl and follows her away from us.

Natalie's brown eyes flash
and she pounces on Melinda.
        "How many times do I have to tell you
        that you shouldn't answer questions?
        Didn't your parents tell you not to talk
        to strangers?"

Melinda shrugs. "At home, we say *hi* to everyone."

"But you're not in Kansas anymore."

"Not Kansas. Louisiana."

Natalie rolls her eyes and clenches her fists.
"I *know*. Just *don't* talk to them."
        Plenty of drama, these two.

On the *Paseo de la Reforma*

Arms linked, we weave through traffic
while packed city buses pump out diesel
exhaust, spill people on every corner.

Cars, ten years older than those at home,
honk, growl, and roar, but none wake
drunks who slump in alleys or doorways
and reek of urine and old sweat,
or distract green-uniformed police,
hands on holsters, at every corner.

The stained stone buildings, enormous,
with imposing black metal gates,
remind me of photos from Europe.
Others have rainbows of broken glass
and jagged metal cemented along the top
of high walls to keep out intruders.

People pack the sidewalks:
copper-skinned workers sweep doorsteps,
unfold awnings, rearrange fruit displays—
mangos, papayas, bananas, limes—
while nuns herd lines of chattering children
past women in *serapes* who pat and flip
tortillas frying in hot oil on small *braseros*.
I love the flower stands the most—
irises, roses, marigolds, zinnias—
an explosion of color more vivid
than any I've ever seen,
like a Disney movie, only better.

Natalie and I Share Our Stories

The sports club is like a fancy resort.
After a swim, Natalie and I lounge
by the outdoor pool
and watch Melinda do laps.
That girl has so much energy.

"So why did your parents send you here?"
Natalie asks, twisting her long, brown hair
into a knot. "Trouble at home?"
I shake my head.

"I've been dreaming of living here
for years."

Natalie quits playing with her hair,
presses together her full, heart-shaped lips
before she asks, "Are you pulling my leg?"

I laugh. "No. When I was little
and went to my dad's company picnic,
I met this girl Alicia whose family
came from Mexico. We had so much fun
together that our parents would drive
us across town to see each other
sometimes on Sundays."

Natalie's brown eyes widen
and she pulls her head back.

"I loved being at her house.
There was always so much
going on— women in the kitchen,
laughing and talking and yelling
at their kids while they made tamales,
men in the backyard with the music going."

Natalie smiles and nods.

"Sometimes we'd go for walks
around this square in her neighborhood
and everyone would be out having fun."

"Not like my neighborhood in Philly,"
Natalie says. "Our house feels like a tomb.
My parents are older, and I'm an only child.
Sometimes I think I make them nervous."

We're silent for a minute, listen
to Melinda's rhythmic splashes
as she swims laps.

It's hard for me to imagine Natalie's life.
My family is loud and argumentative,
but we have the same weird sense of humor
and laugh a lot, even when we're giving
each other a hard time.

"My house isn't that bad," I say.
"Alicia loved coming over,

sitting at my sister's vanity
putting on make-up
or digging through all our books
like she was hunting for treasure.
And she loved my grandma's
matzo ball soup."

"*Matzo* balls?"

I smile. "Jewish version of dumplings."

Natalie studies me,
a look I've seen often.

I hope she isn't looking for horns.

I keep talking, my best defense.
"Anyway, I couldn't wait to visit Mexico.
The way Alicia's *tios* and *tias*
described it, it sounded magical."

Another nod from Natalie.

"Don't you want to be here?" I ask.

"Oh, I like it now," she says,
"but I didn't want to come.
Hated it for a while."

"Why are *you* here?"

"My parents sent me to a Catholic girls' school,"
Natalie says, "but then I met a guy at Woolworth's.
When they found out I had a Protestant boyfriend,
they shipped me off, figured I'd meet
a nice Catholic boy in Mexico."

She snorts. "I can tell by the look on your face
that you don't know many Catholics."

"It's the same for Jews.
Our parents want us to marry our own,
but that doesn't always happen."

"I didn't know that," she says.
"You're the first Jew I've met."

        "I get that a lot," I say.
"I hope I'm not the last."

Am I imagining it, or does she blush?

I keep talking.
"Melinda says you have a boyfriend
so that must make it more fun to be in Mexico."

 "I guess my parents did get *that* right," she says,
"because Javier and I have been dating for months."

"So your Spanish must be really good."

She laughs. "I wish. If it were, I wouldn't
be going to the American University
for lectures in English."

"How do you and Javier talk?"

"Who says we talk?"
Her dimples show when she smiles.
          Even though I smile back,
          my stomach muscles tighten.
          I've never been a flirt
          or had a serious boyfriend.
          Hearing her talk about guys,
          I'm not sure if I'm ready
          for her kind of excitement.

Time for another subject.
"Can you believe the Olympics
are almost here? I can't wait
to meet people from everywhere."

 Natalie flashes a model's white smile,
"I can help with that.
When Javier comes over,
I'll ask him to take us to a club.
We'll meet his university friends."

Melinda walks up then,
shaking her curls like a wet puppy
and spraying water all over us.
"Check out that cute lifeguard,"
she says. "He's so cool."

I leave the two of them talking guys
          and head inside to explore the club.

Steamed

I've never been in one before.
It's so cloudy that I stop inside the door,
feel my way to a tile bench,
touch someone's bare thigh.

I snap my hand back
      and say, *"Disculpeme."*
      The girl laughs softly.

My vision clears.
      I am the only one
      in a swimming suit.

Wrapped in towels,
      the others look my age
      or younger.

"Hey, *gringa*. Is it your first time here?"
a pale girl with blue eyes asks.

I'm sure I am turning red
and not only from the intense heat.
      "Yes, I'm new."

A thin brunette with almond-shaped eyes asks,
"Are you on your honeymoon?"

      "No!"

She readjusts her towel. "How old are you?"

      "I'm almost eighteen."
      And soaked in sweat.

"Here you're almost an old maid.

      "Me?"

Several girls laugh. "We marry at 16 or 17."

      "Are you pulling my leg?"

"No, you did that," laughed the one whose leg

I touched. "The men here like having young wives."

I try not to shudder
when they tell me they marry
men at least ten years older.
They look like American teenagers,
but what do their husbands look like?

They chat among themselves then,
speaking in Spanish so fast that I can't keep up.
Probably they pity me for being alone.
but they are here on a weekday—
so they don't work or go to school.
If they have children, they aren't with them.
They must have maids that watch them.
What do they do all day?
Almost choking now in the suffocating heat.
I smile, wave goodbye, and leave the room.

"*Vaya con Dios*," one calls.

"*You too!*" I answer.

A cool shower washes away the sweat,
but the claustrophobia of their lives,
belonging to older men, lingers.

I wonder if the women back in the steam room
find my life as frightening
as I find theirs.

Guillermo

Our first connection
isn't with words
but with our eyes.
He scans the club
with a curiosity and intensity
that I love,
and he sees me
watching him.

It's not good
for anyone to notice me.

I didn't tell Javier and Natalie
that I'm too young to be in a club,
not even eighteen,
Mexico's legal drinking age.
I step behind a pillar
in a dark corner.

But Guillermo finds me anyway,
surprises me with a *Coca Cola*.
Even his eyes, liquid brown
with specks of amber, smile.
"I'm Guillermo," he says.
"Would you like a drink?"

I feel the blood rush to my face.

He grins. "No alcohol."
How can a stranger read me so well?

My eyes lock with his
as I reach for the cup and taste.

He is telling the truth.
It is only a Coke,
I find my voice.
"*Gracias. Me llamo Diana.*"

He is a student at the Polytechnic,
Javier's acquaintance,
Chango's friend,
one I won't forget.

Revolution

"What brings you to Mexico?" he asks.

"The American university.
The Olympics.
A chance to learn about your culture."
My voice drops.
*Why am I talking like a contestant
in a beauty pageant?*
I wipe my sweaty palms on my skirt.

"You're adventurous," he says.

I smile and nod.
We lean forward across the table,
a flickering candle creating shadows
between us as we move our hands and talk.
Somehow our "Spanglish" works.

"Did you go to Chicago for the protests
at the 1968 Democratic Convention?" he asks.

"No," I say, wondering if he understands
the distances between cities in the U. S.

He nods. "My father would never allow
my sisters to do anything like that."

I frown, draw an X
in the condensation on my glass.
"My parents don't make my decisions.
                                        I make them."

He pulls his head back, sees I'm upset
and raises his hands, palms out.
"Who am I to say what is best for you?"

My face flushes. Am I overreacting
or was he being *macho?*

I scratch my damp napkin.
"I worry about the violence
that breaks out in protests
like the one in Chicago."

Guillermo sits up straighter.
"But everyone is so passionate
and speaks the truth.
Che Guevara says,
'*Los agitadores son la ignorancia,
el hambre y la pobreza.*'"

That much I understand. It means,
"The trouble makers are ignorance,
hunger, and poverty." In the US. too.
But Guevara is a Communist.

Is Guillermo?

"For me," I say,
"'the pen is mightier than the sword.'"

He looks confused.

"I think I can be heard better by writing.
I want to be a photojournalist."

"*Foto...?*"

"Someone who takes pictures..."
I capture him with my imaginary camera,
"and writes about what she sees."

"Oh, so that's why you have a pencil
stuck in your hair. *Ahora entiendo.*"

Oh no. I've done it again.
I'm always sticking pencils and pens
behind my ear so I won't lose them
and I forgot to leave them at home.
I feel my neck flush as I remove it
and tuck it into my purse.

He keeps talking though,
doesn't act like he thinks I'm weird.
"We can make the world a better place."

I point to an Olympic poster
hanging on the window.
"It's the theme of the Olympics, right?
Everything is possible in peace,"

"*Es verdad.*" The truth.

I sigh. "But I can't even vote until I'm twenty-one,
and I'll only be eighteen by the election."

"When is your birthday?" he asks
as the shadows of our hands touch
and I wonder how they feel.
He's so good-looking, slim but muscular,
with light-filled almond-shaped eyes.

"September 24."
I lift my cup, hoping
he can't see my fingers tremble.

Guillermo pushes back a strand
of hair that has fallen over my eye.
"Your birthday is soon."

I look down, feel myself warm
from his touch and wonder
what it would be like to kiss those full lips.
"How are birthdays celebrated here?"

"Wait and see."
And then he takes my hand
and pulls me up to dance.

First Dance

I'm usually stiff and self-conscious,
never was good at following
during high school dances.

But Guillermo places his hand
on my waist and pulls me toward him.
He takes my right hand,
and holds it over his heart.

We are so close that I can smell him.
He smells like a man, earthy, not
like the boys I've danced with before
who reek of aftershave
even when they don't have facial hair.

Maybe it's the throb of the music.
Maybe it's the beat of his heart
beneath our hands.
Maybe it's the thump of desire.
But he is not leading.
I am not following.
We are dancing together.

The Next Day

all I can think about is Guillermo,
how I eased into his arms,
how our bodies molded to each other's
as we danced,

but he didn't ask for my number.
I may never see him again.
It bothers me that it bothers me.

I want to live in a world that's bigger
than one man
        one family
                one house.

Guillermo is a trap
                but
                      it felt so good
                      to be in his embrace.

The Letter I Don't Write Home

Now you can't find me
when breakfast dishes pile high on the counter—
toast crumbs and orange egg yolks paint plates,
my brother's Frosted Flakes cling
to the sides of the cereal bowl
                      he never washes.
Now you can't find me
when I forget to move the wet towels
to the dryer at exactly the right "Mom time"
or fold the sheets so they stack
without toppling in the stuffed linen closet
                      where Dad hides cigarettes.
Now you can't find me
when your need for a babysitter
(so you can have dinner with Mr. and Mrs. Levy)
trumps my plans to go to Mindy Shapiro's party
where Kevin Getz may or may not be
                    waiting in the rec room
                  shadows for a kiss.

Now you can't find me.
                    Sorry.
I'm dancing down packed city sidewalks,
listening to buses growl, peddlers shout,
girls chatter. Chili peppers, pinwheel colors,
trumpeting horns beckon from every direction
and I've never felt
                    more alive.

Teotihuacan: Climbing the Pyramid of the Sun

As we walk the bare Avenue of the Dead
toward the towering Pyramid of the Sun
I wonder how the ancient Aztecs felt
traveling this road to witness sacrifices,
if the sun ravaged them as it does us today.

Natalie stops, pulls out a handkerchief
and wipes sweat from her upper lip.
Melinda and I gulp water from our thermoses.
"Talk about the Gates of Hell," she complains.

"My mother would love it," I say.
"She always has her nose in a book
about ancient civilizations."
I don't say what I think, that it's strange
that she's curious about other places,
but doesn't understand my travel bug.

When we finally reach the base
of the looming pyramid, I look up
and the air whooshes right out of me.
No one told me the steps were steep
and uneven. And I didn't tell anyone
that I'm afraid of heights.

Melinda takes off.
"Race you to the top,"
Natalie laughs, "There are 248 steps.
With her short legs, we'll catch up
by the first platform." She climbs too,
but at a steady pace, looking

over her shoulder to ask,
"Are you coming?"

I hesitate. There's no railing.
The cringing coward inside me screams,
"Don't do it." But I know this is also why
I came to Mexico, to challenge myself,
to find out who I am, what I want, what I can do.

I take a deep breath and climb.
With each step I push back panic,
the knowledge of the growing void behind me.
"One step. One more."
I tell myself, jaws clenched,
bringing my feet together on each stone,
not daring to look down or up
for fear I'll freeze in terror.

In the shimmering heat,
dots appear before my eyes.
Sweat trickles down my sides.
Finally, I reach the first platform
where Melinda waits, breathless.
"Come on, Slow Poke."

"Don't wait for me," I say,
looking only at the next step,
the most my shaky stomach can take.
I wait for my breathing to slow
before I start up again.

As I climb, I think again of Mother,
who smiles when she talks about archaeology,
her mood surprising since she's often distant.
Maybe digging through dirty laundry
and hunting lost shoes buried in my brother's closet
is as miserable for her as heights are for me.
Do her days feel like this, endless climbs?

I finally summon the courage
to look up, sensing the summit
can't be much farther. I can't see
my roommates, who have reached
the top. All I see is the last flight
of steps, inexplicably steeper, narrower,
fit only for birds to roost.

How? How can I make it to the top?
"Breathe," I tell myself. "Just breathe."
Head down to avoid the gaping panorama,
I side-step up them. "Almost there."
I tell myself on every one
of the last fifty-one stairs.

Finally, I am on top,
a blissfully flat plateau,
not intimidating as long as
I'm not right next to the edge.

The view is spectacular;
Mexico unfolds before me.

Light-headed with relief,
I join a tour group to listen
to a guide explaining bloody Aztec
sacrifices offered here centuries ago.

Ball games were at the foot of the pyramid
a battle between the Sun god and Moon god,
day versus night. Some say the ball
represented the skulls of sacrificed victims,
argue about whether winners or losers gave
their lives, an honor for those who offered
themselves. Sounds worse than Vietnam.

Forcing myself to make the climb
was definitely worth it,
but under the fiery sun,
with smoldering stones beneath our feet,
Natalie, Melinda, and I soon retreat
to the treacherous steps.

My breath catches when I realize
going down is much harder than coming up.
Even my roommates hesitate.

Melinda says, "If the Aztecs were so civilized,
why couldn't they have thought up handrails?"

Natalie tucks damp strands of hair behind her ears.
"Maybe it will help if we link arms."

"Oh, no." I put a hand on my stomach.

"If one of us falls, we'll pull everyone down.
We need someone to notify our parents if we die."
They laugh, but I'm not kidding. I'm clammy,
my breath ragged, fighting total panic again.
I focus only on their heads, right in front of me,
so the descent won't defeat me.

Halfway down, Natalie stumbles.
I see her pitch forward, hear her gasp
and grab her arm from behind,
holding her until she steadies herself again.

Melinda *doesn't* hold back.
"Damn Aztecs and their little feet!
These steps are way too narrow."

"Side-steps," I suggest.
Hearts pounding, we try again.
After an eternity in limbo, we reach the base
where the bloody ball games were once played.
I'm exhausted, but triumphant.
Unlike many of the Aztec virgins, we survived.

For Diana the Huntress

Is it possible to fall in love
        at first sight
                with a statue?

I wait across the street
for the university shuttle
but all I see is Diana,
my mythical namesake
and Guardian of Chapultepec Park.

Her sculpted bronze body
is as curved as the bow she holds,
its sharpened arrow pointing
north, shooting stars,
hunting beasts, guarding
El Paseo de la Reforma,
Walkway to Freedom.

Hair flowing in mist
from tiered fountains,
Diana is my compass,
directing me to all
things unexplored,
waiting to be hunted.

I Am Diana

In the myths
there's always a cost for the quest,
a flaw in the character
whose story ends in tragedy.

What will it cost me
to be as free as Diana?

Maybe I'll be frightened.
Maybe I'll be lonely.
Maybe I'll be damaged.
Maybe I'll be ordinary.

Will I be the hunted
or the hunter?

Paradise U.

The university looks like a hillside resort
with a tiny frame post office at its center.
Terraced sidewalks lead down to offices
and up to a line of classrooms with doors open
to a common sidewalk lined with benches
where we can sun ourselves,
waiting for the next class.
                              Every day is spring.
Circular white benches surround trees with
ivy trailing up trunks. Daisies fill window boxes
while marigolds and sweet alyssum
                              border sculptures.

A journalism student, I check out the Press Room
with its floor to ceiling bay window
overlooking a deep wooded ravine.
Two lines of desks face one another
in the building's center. Before each chair,
          a manual typewriter ready for action.

Lunch here means American food.
Bacon and tomato sandwiches on toast.
French fries. Tuna salad. Spaghetti.
But it's nothing like an ordinary school cafeteria.

There's an enormous mural of a *paisano* offering
a basket of bread to two kneeling workers.
People say that Diego Rivera and Frida Kahlo
entertained Leon Trotsky here on the lower road.
          I wonder if Rivera painted this.

Perpendicular to the dining hall
is a wall of windows two stories high.
We can take our trays through French doors
to a terrace with views of snow-covered volcanoes
          Popocatepetl and Iztaccihuatl.

Those high school years in Texas,
stuck in steamy third floor classrooms
with shades covering every window?
This makes it
                    worth every minute.

Popo y Izta

Aztec myths tell their love story:
A mighty ruler insists that Popocatepetl,
a brave warrior, must bring
back a vanquished enemy's head
in order to win permission
to marry his beautiful daughter
Princess Iztacchihuatl, "The White Woman"
in the native Nahua language.

After Popocatepetl leaves on his quest,
a rival falsely informs Iztacchihuatl's
father that the warrior has failed
in his pursuit and died.

Overcome by sorrow, Iztacchihuatl
pines away, dying of a broken heart
before Popocatepetl returns in triumph.

In despair at the news of his lover,
he carries the princess to the mountains,
where he builds a funeral pyre
for both of them. There he also dies.

The gods, touched by their love,
turn them into towering mountains,
the second and third highest in Mexico,

where Izta rests on her back,
an extinct volcano with head,
breasts, knees, and feet
rising in snowy peaks.
Connected by a mountain pass,
Popo sits beside her,
his sporadic exhalations of ash,
reminders of his eternal love.

They're the first volcanoes I've ever seen.
I'm wowed by their blue-white beauty,
but annoyed by the usual myth,
another love story that ends in senseless death.

First Letters

Most people have parents
who want to drive them to college.
Mine didn't even drive me to the airport.
I drove my Rambler to a hotel, parked it,
took the shuttle, and found my own way
through international travel.

Mother wrote me a letter the very same day,
complaining about having to pick up the car,
and how she was so distracted
by my leaving that she burned supper.

Dad wrote the next day, fussing at me,
"That was Mother's pink pillow, loaned
to Libby for the summer, you fink!"

I didn't pack a pink pillow.
And if it was good enough
for my sister, the bride,
why isn't it good enough for me?

The bigger truth comes out later in the letter.
He feels lost without "my two lovely daughters."
I know my parents are asking themselves
what they will do without us,
but I doubt they are asking
how I will do without them.
I have been taking care of myself
for a long, long time.

Mirror, Mirror

I have left my parents' house of mirrors
where I grew up seeing our faces, knowing
I was theirs, but unlike my sister,
mesmerized by her own reflection,
I avoided my own.

I have my mother's wavy chestnut hair,
a fair face, round green eyes, full lips.
I'm pretty enough in an ordinary way,

but I don't want to be like Mother
                              or Libby.
What matters most to them
is what people see,
what others say about us.
I care about what we do.

In high school, I volunteered
once a week, wrote newsletters
at a community center
in a rundown neighborhood.
As usual, Mother didn't approve.
She said, "Charity begins at home."

I left much unsaid,
secrets that sometimes
                              up.
                    me
        eat

Here's one:
I love my family,
but sometimes...

        I don't like them,
        not one little bit.

        If they weren't my family,
        I doubt I'd choose them for friends.

Now I can run
        from those who confine me,
                all the while calling me their own.

Surprise!

One evening Javier, Chango, and Guillermo
        drop by for a visit.
We don't want snoopy Señora Salinas
        to listen in
and we're always looking for an escape
so we jump when the guys suggest
                we go for a walk.

Outside, Chango opens a paper sack
full of warm *sopapillas*
his *abuelita* made for us.
Our hands come out of the bag
covered in confectioner's sugar.

The sweet dough melts in our mouths,
as we chase each other down streets
where car horns blare like mariachis
and the air smells of cigarette smoke,
frying tortillas, and *limones*.

The boys threaten to use our skirts
as napkins. As we round a corner,
I glare at Guillermo, and make two fists.

He does the same, then blocks my way,
and brushes his thumb against my cheek.
"More sugar," he says, and licks the sugar
from his finger. "Sweet like you."

I laugh
because we both know that's not true,
but those intense eyes hold me captive
and the world falls away.

¿Peligro?

We walk into a *tienda,*
and cruise the aisles while
I practice food names.
"Naranjas, limones, manzanas.
Oranges, lemons, apples."
I point out other fruits.
"Hah, *mango* and *papaya*!
En ingles y español."

He holds my hand up
in the victory position
and I move closer to him,
hoping he won't let go.

He doesn't.
He wraps his arm around me

and all I can think about
is how it would feel
to embrace him, face-to-face.

Our eyes lock and we move
to a far corner of the store,
where we startle an old couple,
a bent man leaning on a cane.
His wife is upright but her skin
is as withered as a leaf in fall.
She draws in a sharp breath
and mutters something.

Guillermo pulls me aside,
and says, *"Discúlpanos,
por favor"* and I say,
"Perdóneme."

The woman moans and
disappears up an aisle,
leaving the man eying us
while rooted to his spot.

Guillermo nods and we walk
around him to a washtub
full of canned drinks buried in ice.
He pulls out two dripping colas
and hands me one.
Our fingers touch, icy
and warm, wet and dry.

That's when the wrinkled woman
reappears and hands a paper bag to Guillermo.
"¡Cuidado! ¡Veo sangre!"
Her voice sounds like sandpaper
rubbed across a splintered board.

At her warning,
he drops my hand
and shifts from foot to foot.

"Escúchame," she insists.
*"Pon esto huevo debajo de tu cama.
Se extenderá el mal.
Luego entierra el huevo mañana."*

At first I think I've misunderstood her
when she tells him to put an egg under his bed.
It will absorb the bad, the danger she sees.
She says he should bury the egg in the morning.
She must be *loca,* crazy.

But Guillermo listens, accepts the bag
and walks her away from me
as they speak in Spanish too rapid
for me to understand. He thanks her.
She shakes her drooping head
and blinks wet eyes
as we quickly pay and exit.

Clouds gather overhead
and the afternoon heat presses
on our shoulders,
the air unexpectedly hard to breathe.
The electricity between us is gone.

I turn to Guillermo
whose lips are tight
and shoulders tense.
"What just happened?
There's something here
I'm missing."

"*No te preocupes. No es nada.*"
His head is down.
so I can't see his eyes.

I feel like a deflated balloon,
like the worst *gringa* of them all.
"I need your help to understand
your culture. What aren't you
telling me?"

He hesitates but finally looks up,
meeting my eyes. "*Bueno, pero*
it's an old custom. The egg is supposed
to protect me from curses or bad luck."

"Has it ever worked for you?"

He shrugs. "My mother swears it saved me
when I was three and had a high fever.

After she buried the egg,
I got better."

To me this is a silly superstition,
but a new fear chases away that thought.
"Wait." I stop and put my hand
on his arm. "Did the woman think
I would hurt you?"

The corners of his mouth turn up,
but only slightly.
"No. Nothing like that.
She kept muttering about eagles
flying through a storm with guns
and it raining blood.
She didn't make any sense."

I take a deep breath. "Oh,
Maybe she has Old Timers."

"Es possible," he says.

If it's possible, why
does he look so serious?

Thunder rumbles in the distance.
We pick up the pace,
rush down sidewalks,
trying to beat the rain home.

A peddler wrapped in a *serape*
maneuvers his cart under an awning
and stops abruptly in front of Guillermo
who bumps into it.

Emotions flood Guillermo's face—
he looks surprised, confused, afraid.
I look down, see thick, clear liquid
ooze from the paper sack's bottom
onto the sidewalk. The raw egg.

I take the dripping bag from him
and put it in a trash can outside
a cafe. "Don't worry," I say.
"You can get another egg."

He nods and smiles,
but there are worry lines
across his forehead.

As we reach the apartment,
the sky opens up,
pelting us with rain.

I wonder if I should worry
about a broken egg.

Earthquake

On Friday night I wake up
because my bed is shaking
                              again.
Damn subway construction.
Or maybe it's that voice in my ear,
whispering my name
                              over and over.
I swim up from the depths of dreams
as Melinda touches my arm.

"Sorry," she says,
                    trembling so hard
she's shaking the soft bed.

"He   was   all   over   me."

That woke me up. "What? Who?"

She's crying now.

                    "That lifeguard
from the *deportivo*.
                    It's all my fault."

There's just enough light from the window
          to see her crumpled silhouette.

I sit up, reach for her, touch bare skin,
then her half-slip and shiver.
                    Where is her dress?

She jerks back like my fingers are on fire.

Now my heart is pounding too.
"What happened?" I whisper.

　　　"I said no.
　　　　　He said American girls
　　　　　　　　　　　play hard to get.
　　　　He tried to　　　make　　　me."

She squeezes the words out
like each one is a blow.

Reality knifes through the darkness.
All I can hear are Melinda's ragged breaths.

"Oh-my-God!"

　　"Natalie warned me," Melinda says. "She
said
　　　　　　　　　　　if you ask a guy
　　　　to take you to the mountains
　　　　　　　to see the city lights,
you're
　　　just　　asking　for　　　it.
　　I thought that was something silly
her mother　　told her.　　I didn't believe it."

I take her cold hands in mine.
Sometimes Melinda doesn't understand
the most obvious things. I say,
"At home some boys think
'going to see the city lights'
means 'let's make-out.'"

　　　　　Melinda yanks her hands from mine.
　　　　　"He wanted a lot more than that!"

I shiver. *Did he rape her
and she's not admitting it?
　　　Should I wake the Señora?*
I wipe my hands on my nightgown.

"But I kneed him," she says,
　　　　　"and jumped out of the car."

Then the words rush out. "I was afraid he'd be angry and chase after me, and it was so dark that I could have fallen off the ridge. I've never been so scared in my life."

She's shivering again so I pull the blanket
from the bed and wrap it around her.
"When he heard me crying,
he asked me
to get back in the car,
kept asking, *'Por que?'*

At first I couldn't move. But then
the rock,
the stick."

I jump up and reach for the light.
"Did he beat you?"

"Stop." She knocks my hand away from the switch.
"You'll wake Natalie.
You don't understand.
I got down on my knees
and   felt   around   on   the   ground
for   a sharp   rock and a thick   stick.
so I could fight
if he came near me again.
I threatened him
before I got in the back seat.

He called me
a *gringa loca*
and drove me back.
The whole way I couldn't remember
a single word of Spanish.
It was the longest ride of my life."

I hug her. This time she lets me.
"Where's your dress?"

"He tore it when he   grabbed me
so I put it in the bathroom trash."

I say, *"Señora* will find it in there
and will ask lots of questions."

"I wasn't thinking.   Just wanted it off.
Don't ever want to see it again."

"I'll put it in my book bag," I say,
"and give it to a beggar tomorrow."

Then I tuck her into bed and whisper,
"Everything will look better in the morning."
I sound like my mother, but, somehow,
                                        the words fit.

The building shakes again, rattling the windows.
From the vase on the windowsill,
a single purple iris falls to the floor.

Moving Day

Suitcases fill Chango's VW.
No room for Melinda or anyone else.
Javier and Guillermo escort us as we walk
from Sra. Salina's cramped, vibrating apartment
across the busy *Reforma* to our new residence.

We half-run, hard to do in our dresses
and pumps, but we have a bet going,
who can get there the fastest through traffic,
Chango or the walkers.

Laughing, Guillermo grabs my hand
as we dart around cars and buses,

hurry past the butcher shops, bakeries,
and flower stands on the other side.

Many of the stores here look like garages
with metal doors that roll up in the morning.
They stay open throughout the day
so that smells of yeast and mangos,
grilled meat and tortillas tempt us at every turn.

As we rush by a shoe repair,
a man with coarse black hair
growls at me, "*Puta.*"

Guillermo stops, spins around and shouts,
"What did you say?"

Oh, no, no, no.
Men fight over less.

"Let's go," I say, tugging on his arm. "It's okay.
Didn't you see the puckered look on his face?
He was spitting in the street."

Guillermo's whole body is tense,
like an animal ready to strike.
I let go of his arm
and scowling,
he faces me.

But then he locks me in his unwavering gaze
and sees,
             sees
                          what I see.

"It's okay. Really," I say.
"We have a bet to win."
I move away, and hope he follows.

                          HE DOES!

Chango Wins

He's leaning against the car,
listening to his transistor radio
like he's been there for hours,
but my hand on the hot hood
tells a different story.

So we girls owe him a picnic
in Chapultepec Park
on Sunday afternoon.
We invite Javier and Guillermo too.

That settled, we buzz in at the gate.
Sr. and Sra. Padilla let us in.
Of course the first rule—
no males in our rooftop room—
goes into effect right away.

We visit with the Padillas
while the boys carry our bags
up and leave them
outside our door.

When they are finished,
we go into the foyer
where Guillermo is sitting
at the telephone desk, writing
something on the rubber trim
that lines the soles of his canvas sneakers.
He puts his hand over what he's written,
flashes a smile, and says
a few quiet words to the *señor.*

Under the Padilla's watchful eyes,
we walk the boys to the gate.
Javier and Natalie hold hands,
Guillermo and I walk side-by-side
electricity arcing as we brush
hands with each step.

Melinda, still frightened
from her trip up the mountain,
stays a foot away from
a very confused Chango.
I feel sorry for both of them.

New Residence

We enter our new home
through a plain brown door on the roof,
but inside our room is sunny,
with rust-colored tile floors, storage,
and a private bath. My favorite—
the sets of sliding glass doors across one wall
that lead to a balcony, magenta bougainvillea
spilling from its blue boxes.
It's private and perfect and ours.

From the Roof...

we see antenna,
but I haven't watched TV
since I arrived.
Fine with me.

In Texas I saw
nuclear mushrooms eclipse the sun,
Watts burn to ash in six days,
John, MLK, Bobby die in gunfire's rapid bursts,
helicopters whir our guys in and out of Viet Nam,
Chicago police batter protestors with their batons.
Screens showed a world choked
by hatred's flames and smoke.

Here in Mexico, without TV,
                                        I live in color,
reality more black and white
                                        and red all over.

Carolina

The Padillas have a maid
who at fourteen left her family
to cook and clean here.
She lives off the kitchen
in a tiny room with cement floors.

Outside our suite on the roof
is a concrete, cold water sink
where Carolina washes clothes
and hangs them on clotheslines
crisscrossing the roof's length.

Sometimes at night
when all the clothes
have been scrubbed,
the beds sheets turned down,
floors mopped,
rugs vacuumed,
dishes washed,
she slips upstairs to visit with us,

the only other teenagers in the house.

She stands with her back to the space
heater to warm herself.
I wonder how cold and damp
it is in her tiny room.

She pulls her thick waist length hair
over one shoulder, says her father
will cut it off and sell it when she visits
her *pueblo*, and then she'll grow it again.

Her sweet spirit reminds me
of my unearned good fortune:
to be born in a different place
with parents who allow me so much freedom
and would never sell any part of me.

First College Exam

As we open our bluebooks,
        a classmate appears at the door.
Through the glass we see him,
        mumbling, trembling, wild-eyed, pale,
holding up a bleeding hand
        from a window he broke.

The professor leads him away,
                        to where?

Someone says,
        "A bad trip, maybe mescaline."

I feel sick to my stomach, put down my pen,
        to wipe my sweaty hands on my skirt.

There's no one here to rescue us—
        no counselors, doctors, resident advisors
                        on our commuter campus.
        No student services.
We're totally on our own,
                        unprotected.

The boy's voiceless terror

ricochets off the classroom walls
as my fingers fist around my pen
and I try to focus on answers to questions
about Octavio Paz, his *Labyrinth of Solitude.*

Sunday Picnic

When Spring visits Texas,
its unseen hand dabs green
paint on budding trees.
Branches stretch, touch sky blue,
a masterpiece never lasting
more than a few days.

But spring is every day in Chapultepec Park.
Sunlit leaves flicker from jade to silver
against a background of white clouds.

My friends and I unfold our blankets
on the grass, spread out our picnic:
bolillos, queso blanco, jicama,
salted peanuts, mangos, *churros*, bottled water.
Javier, Chango, and Guillermo bring *Dos Equis.*

We are all in our Sunday best:
As the guys loosen their ties
and remove their sweaters, we tug
on our skirts for maximum coverage.
I'm grateful the blanket protects our nylons.
But the confining clothes don't bother us.
Nothing does.

While we eat, we play a game.
Each of us picks a color.
We count how many children pass us
with helium balloons in that shade.
Whoever picks the most popular one
gets to choose the next activity.
When my red wins, I ask for photos.

I pull out my Canon camera
and my new friends pose:
playing kick the beer can on a *futbol* field,
tromping over a wooden bridge

bordered by fields of yellow marigolds,
licking the sugary cinnamon from our lips
as we feed each other *churros*.

Guillermo stops a young man
walking with his girlfriend
and asks him to take a picture
of the group and then one of the two of us.

We split up to explore the park,
agreeing to meet back at 4:00.
Guillermo and I take a gravel path
lined with hot pink dahlias.
His rough hand, warm and strong,
encloses mine. I smile at him,
intertwining my fingers
with his, loving the connection.

Truth or Dare

On a bench in front of a fountain,
we sit and talk. "There's a game
we play in Texas," I say.
"I ask you a question.
You have to answer with the truth,
or accept punishment."

He asks, "What's the punishment?"

"Mmm. Let's see. Loser has to run
around the fountain twenty-five times?"

"Bueno, but I ask first."

"Okay," I say.
"My life is an open book."

"The man from the shoe repair
on your street, did he spit
at you or curse you?"

I feel the blood rush to my face.
I don't want him to confront *Puta* Man.
Should I run around the fountain?

No, either way he'll figure out my lie.
Clever question.

"He cursed *and* spit," I say,
"but please don't let it upset you.
He doesn't even know me
so I don't care what he thinks."

Guillermo takes my hands and looks
into my eyes, sending the butterflies
in my stomach into their usual frenzied flutter.
"Diana, please stay away from this man,
                    walk on *el otro lado*.
Someone who is so angry with strangers
can be dangerous. People can surprise you
                    in a bad way."

This is new too, someone other than my parents,
telling me to be careful. I love his concern,
but does he think of me as a little sister,
someone who needs his protection?
Maybe I should stay away from Guillermo.

"My turn.
What did you write on your shoe at the Padillas?"

He crosses his legs so I can see the inside
of his canvas shoe. "*Reconoces esto?*"
On it are a series of numbers
that look familiar, but I can't place them.
I shrug and shake my head no.

He laughs.
"Your telephone number."
Then I do something
I've never done before,
that I shouldn't do now.
I lean forward and kiss him,
right on his delicious full lips.
A taste of cinnamon lingers there.

When I realize what I have done,
I pull back and put my hand
                    over my mouth.
At home guys have kissed me,
but I have never made the first move.
I raise my eyes to Guillermo's.

With his eyes open wide
and his lips slightly parted,
he looks surprised too,
but he must not mind because
he takes my face in his gentle
hands and kisses me back,
his soft lips leaving me breathless.

Music from the carousel cuts through
our silence. I pull him to his feet.
"Better go back," I say, but I wish
those kisses could last forever.

Good No More

Natalie's voice runs through my head.
"Mexican men see women
as virgins or whores."
Is she right?

Will Guillermo think
I'm a whore when I'm a virgin
and don't want to be either?

With two kisses,
I may have ruined
my reputation
and scared away Guillermo.

On the Path

We see an old couple,
the man bent almost in half
steadied by a cane.
They walk toward us.

Guillermo's hand tightens
on mine and he stops,
suggests we try a new path,
but it's too late;
the woman from the store sees us.

The leathery lines on her face
frame her sudden grimace
and her shrill voice carries

across the short distance
between us.

"¡Peligro! ¡Peligro!
¡Ten cuidado!" she shrieks.
"Yo lo veo. La oscuridad.

Guillermo calls to her,
"Si, te escucho.
Entiendo." He nods to her husband.
"No te preocupes. Estoy bien."

Then he pulls me away
and we walk quickly
in the other direction.

Her cries of *"¡Peligro!*
¡Cuidado!" echo behind us.

At the gates. I ask,
"Why does she think you're in danger?"

Guillermo shakes his head
and wipes the line of sweat
from his top lip.
"She sees things."

"Did you put an egg under your bed?"

He looks down at his canvas sneakers
and shakes his head.

"Maybe you should."

As we join our friends,
I still wonder,
Am I the danger she sees?

Eighteenth Birthday

Bouquets of roses arrive at breakfast.
My roommates and the guys must have bought out
the flower stand at *Calles Milton y Copernico*
where roses sell for a dollar a dozen.
By late afternoon eighteen dozen have arrived.

Vases fill the Padillas' flat
and the smell of roses drifts up the stairwell
to our room where there are flowers
of every color, roses everywhere.

Sr. and Sra. have birthday cake
and invite the boys.
We sit around their big table,
where everyone sings *Cumpleanos Feliz*.
I make a wish and blow out my candles,
and then we feast on *tres leches*,
lick pecan sprinkled icing from our forks
while the Padillas smile proudly at us
as if they were our own parents.

Card from My Father

"Be a good girl—
you have finally made it to eighteen,
YOU OLD MAID!"

My father thinks he's funny.
I do not.

Someday,
someday,
I will find the courage
to ask him why.
If he loves my sister
and me so much,
why
is he in such a big hurry
for us to marry?

3:30 AM

I don't know which of us wakes first,
but Melinda, Natalie, and I are not dreaming
when we hear mariachi melodies.

In our nightgowns, we slide open the doors,
go out on the balcony for a final surprise.
In the street below, Guillermo, Javier, Chango

and two other musicians serenade us
with *Las Mañanitas,* a Mexican birthday song.

The crisp night fills with the musky scent of roses.
Yearning notes rise, songs of distance and longing.
We do what young women on balconies always do—
ignore the thorns that tear our tender fingertips
and toss down the flowers with their velvet petals.
Crimson, pink, white, yellow. They float down
to our beloveds, along with our desires.

Learning Verbs

Melinda and I sit across from each other,
islands in a sea of Spanish textbooks and notebooks.

She sighs, "I've been out with Chango twelve times
He asks for *besos* and looks so sad when I say no.
I don't know if I'm scared to kiss him after the city
lights nightmare or if he just doesn't turn me on,
but after so many dates, I feel like I owe him.

"But if you don't like him..."

"Oh, I do like him. I just don't *like* him like him."

In some strange way, what she says make sense.
Melinda asks, "What about you and Guillermo?"

"I definitely like him like him.
Usually I feel more like you, more 'ew' than 'wow,'
but when Guillermo kisses me,
I never want to stop."

I never expected to be that girl, the one
that thinks about a boy all the time
so I'm surprised when I say, "In Spanish,
there are so many ways to say, 'I love you.'"

We say them back and forth to each other:
"Me encanta."

"Te amo."

"Te quiero."

"Te adoro."

"Con carino..."

"Me gustan tus besos."

"No me gustan tus besos."

"Ay, no mas!"

Chapultepec Park: September 25, 1968

Like Diego Rivera's *Flower Seller,* a brown woman
kneels next to baskets of lilies, irises, sunflowers.
      I buy an armful, remember Guillermo's kiss
      as I walk through Chapultepec Park
      among the *helado* vendors,
      pinwheel spinners, *futbol* players.
Red and yellow balloons snare
      running children in their dangling strings.

I follow a winding path to a sculpture garden
where sun-warmed statues embrace in a vacuum.

Like a shadow, silence fills the plaza.
An absence of sound pulls me
from a flower-filled reverie.

      I catch my breath, dart down a path
to the broad *Paseo de la Reforma*, the avenue

deserted. No rattling cars, smoke-belching buses,
        shawl-draped women
           with bundles and babies.

Stiff-legged soldiers goose step in tight rows,
rifles, bayonets, bazookas against their shoulders.
Thump thump, thump thump, thump thump.

At road's curve, tanks roll,
      mechanical monsters, geared,
      devour everything
           in their path.

I run.

My sandals slap the tender undersides
of my bare feet

as   weave   and   of   straight
   I   in   out   razor   lines,

blank-faced soldiers, blinded by command.

My heart
pounds like
their thumping boots.

I tear across the avenue,
trailing torn lilies, bruised irises,
crushed sunflowers.

I Run

never stop,

even when

smog fills my lungs,

there's a stitch in my side,

my eyes sting with tears.

I swerve to miss an abandoned newsstand,

knock mangos from a deserted fruit cart,

dart around empty cars parked on side streets.

Dots appear before my eyes,

and I can't catch my breath.

My fear mutes *Puta* Man's shout

from his shoe repair shop.

Too frantic to buzz for entry,

I scale the Padilla's gate,

drop what's left

of my flowers to find my key,

open the door, and

collapse on the stairs,

sides heaving.

STUPID

       stupid,
               stupid

to stay behind
       in the park
               alone

after only weeks in Mexico,
       when I still understand little about the culture.

Stupid,
       stupid,
               stupid

to stay
       there
               alone

simply because I'm always so determined
               to do
                   what I want
                       when I want.

I thought I was so grown up,
                   so smart.
                       I was wrong.

Peligro!

I can't tell Natalie what happened in the park.
She'll point out the obvious,
that girls in Mexico only travel
with chaperones or in groups.

I do tell Melinda, who asks,
"Why are you so freaked out?
Guys love guns. We walk around
with them all the time in Louisiana.
Come hunting with me and my brother sometime.
It's fun. Then you won't be so scared."

I drop my head, knowing
she can't understand my raw fear,
how sure I am the soldiers' feet
were pounding out a warning,
that bad times are coming,
and no one is safe.

If she had seen their faces,
maybe then she'd understand
the soldiers weren't hunting for sport;
their prey was human.

I Dream

Rose petals, teardrops rain
down, encircling Guillermo
in a swirling mist.

The downpour
becomes a barrage of bullets.
With each clap of thunder,
he jerks, fades, awash in red.

I awake tasting copper—
metallic, salty, sweet—
my throat inflamed
from unshed screams.

When we dream in Spanish
we celebrate a bilingual milestone,
our immersion into Mexican culture,
but this dream is one I'll never celebrate.

No Sanctuary

The next day I can't wait to go
to the Press Room. It feels like home—
the smells of ink and carbon paper,
sounds of tapping keys,
chatter from open-eyed people.

I want to ask the other journalism students
if they know why soldiers are moving
into the heart of the city,
why Mexicans run from their own troops,
but everyone is distracted,
upset by our editor's news.

Yesterday a car slammed into his wife
when she was bicycling.
Even though she had broken ribs,
she was put in jail and officials sent
the Mexican driver home.

Maybe the authorities hope for a pay-off,
think the editor and his wife are rich Americans,
but Sam is a Vietnam veteran supporting
his family on the GI bill
and working on the newspaper
so he can attend college tuition free.

The faculty advisor tells him to go to the embassy
to ask for medical help and her release,
but warns it may take weeks. Sam has no money
to speed things up, so we all chip in what we can.

I look through the bay window
that overlooks a mountain gorge.
Today the cozy space feels as fragile
as our first apartment during an earthquake,
like, at any moment, the newsroom could fall
from its perch on the cliff
                        and tumble
                                onto the rocks below.

Encounters with Strangers

Melinda and I wait in line
to buy Olympic tickets.
Ahead of us a turbaned man

from Afghanistan
engages us in conversation
about the coming games.

I'm in reporter heaven,
peppering him with questions
about his culture, but when
I pull out the pencil hiding
in my hair and open my journal,
he turns his back to us.

Another man approaches then,
says he's a reporter too,
from the Soviet Union.

Melinda, open-mouthed,
asks if he's a real Communist.

"Of course," he answers, smiling.

"Why?" she asks.

He ignores her response and shakes his head.
"Ah, Americans. Are you a students here?"

"Yes."

"What do you think about the student
demonstrations at the university?"

Oh, no. I see his buddy is filming us.
Red flags wave.

"We are guests in the country
and have no opinion."
I grab Melinda's arm.
"Come on. Line's shorter over there."

"No, It Isn't," she says.

I pinch her and keep moving.
 "They were filming us,"
I whisper. "I don't want my face
to end up on a propaganda tape
with someone else's voice dubbed in
saying God knows what."

Realization dawns, and Melinda says,

"My parents would have heart attacks."

"Mine too," I say.
"Fifty years ago my grandpa escaped
from Russia and never went back."

"It's settled then. Two tickets to any event
where the U.S. can beat their butts."

Passing

thoughts of the armed soldiers
and lurking Communists
stalk me whenever I walk alone.
Since Melinda is a sophomore
and Natalie is a junior, we have
different schedules and can't always
be together so I have a new goal:
to walk city streets undetected,
looking Mexican so I can blend in
with random groups of girls.

Maybe I can pull it off.
I have thick, medium length
brown hair that flips up at my shoulders.
I'm letting it grow longer
so it will hang straighter.
My eyes are a touch too round,
but eyeliner and eye shadow can fix that.
And although fair, my skin is more ivory
than peaches and cream.
Maybe I can pass as someone
of Spanish descent.

But even if I pass those tests
                there's everything else about me.
Can I hide my American boldness?
I have to remind myself to look down,
never make eye contact with approaching
boys or men, to mask my emotions,
hide everything like the natives,
and to never, ever reveal my curiosity.

I didn't come here to hide,
but now I *want* to hide
in plain sight.

Melinda Slams the Door

to our rooftop room
when she returns from a ride
with Chango and his buddies.

"We were having such a good time
driving through the *Politecnico*
where the guys go to college,
but then they freaked out
when I snapped a few photos of guards."
She waves around her Instamatic Camera.
"I'm a tourist. Of course I take pictures!"

"That's strange," I say, "unless you were taking
photos of something you weren't supposed to see."

"I love it when you talk like a journalist," she says
as she flops down on her bed and sighs.
"Chango snatched the camera right out of my hands,
put it in his pocket, and wouldn't give it back to me
until we got home."

I drop my textbook "Melinda, I told you
how scary the armed troops were.
Everyone else on the streets vanished,
except for me, the dumb *gringa*.
Chango may know something we don't.
Maybe the guards aren't protecting students.
Maybe they're there to control them."
Melinda studies my face, nods,
 and jumps to her feet.
"I know just what you're talking about."
Then she picks up her air guitar and breaks
into a Buffalo Springfield song:

There's something happening here
What it is ain't exactly clear
There's a man with a gun over there
Telling me I got to beware

She points her invisible guitar at an invisible man.

I think it's time we stop, children, what's that sound
Everybody look what's going down

Her hand shades her eyes as she looks around,
and my lips twitch.

There's battle lines being drawn
Nobody's right if everybody's wrong
Young people speaking their minds
Getting so much resistance from behind

When she slaps her butt, I break down and laugh.
No stopping her when she gets like this.
I jump up and join her.

We're waving our arms like lunatics
when Natalie walks in.

Natalie drops her book bag and watches,
straight-faced, as we cover our eyes again.

Paranoia strikes deep
Into your life it will creep
It starts when you're always afraid
You step out of line,
                    the man come and take you away.

Even when Melinda points at me, looks at Natalie,
and twirls her finger in a crazy sign,
I can't stop laughing. We all sing the chorus.
We better stop, hey, what's that sound
Everybody look what's going down.

Tequila

Friday night Guillermo, Javier,
and Chango invite us to a club
in *Polanco*, far from the universities
and close to home. They say it's time
for me to learn how Mexicans drink.

We sit around a wooden table
in a cave-like club with stone walls
and exposed beams overhead.
Javier plucks his guitar as we wait.

The waiters bring small plates
of coarse salt and lime wedges,
then shot glasses with small amounts

of liquid, clear as water.

"This is how," Guillermo says,
turning his left hand sideways
with his thumb to his forefinger.
He places the salt on the flat
side of his hand and loops
the lime wedge over one finger.

Guillermo licks the salt,
tosses back the tequila,
and sucks on the lime.

I'm more interested in his salty
citrus lips than the drink,
but I give it a go.
Lick, swallow (a little), suck.

"You almost have it," Chango says.
"Watch me." He licks,
swallows the whole shot,
gasps, slams down the glass,
sucks on the lime. His runaway eyebrows
shoot up and his face turns red.
He always makes us laugh.

Javier disappears for a few minutes
and the band breaks into "Tequila!"

We sing with them, thump
shot glasses on the table.

I take it slower than Chango—
my sister once got smashed
on one Bloody Mary
and I don't want to act like an idiot.

Good thing too.
Like many things in Mexico,
tequila sneaks up on you.

Walking Home

We eye the crowded VW
Chango and Melinda in the front seats,
Javier and Natalie in the back.

I'm kind of woozy and the breeze
feels good. "Can we walk back, Guillermo?"

"As long as you stay *cerca de mi*," he says
and wraps his arm around my waist.
He gestures for Chango to move on.
Chango gives him a thumbs up.

I laugh. "Smooth." He doesn't
understand my word usage, but
translates my moving closer.
At first we're quiet, enjoying
the night and each other.

Then I begin to talk, telling
him about the editor and his family.
His easy smile vanishes.

"Es muy malo. People here disappear.
He's fortunate to be American
and have a voice."

"So you think the embassy will help?"

"I hope so."
That's when I notice that he is walking
                    us from streetlight to streetlight,
only on the busiest possible streets,
that he's careful where he stops.

I could never admit to him
that I stayed behind in Chapultepec Park,
it was a stupid thing to do,
or that I panicked
and ran through troop lines,
but if I'm careful, maybe I can
ask him about the Soviets.

"Another strange thing," I say,
"maybe you can explain it to me."

He nods.

"A classmate at UA said a Russian
photographer and reporter approached her.
When she used English to tell them to stop
filming her, they asked her what she thought
of students here rallying for change.

She said that she was a visitor
and not involved in Mexican politics."

"Bueno," he said. "Soviets have been talking
to many students, encouraging change,
but they can't know what's best for Mexico.
People in Russia have difficult lives too
so I don't know what makes them experts.*"*

"You're right," I say. "I'm beginning to realize
how lucky I've been."

"Life is hard here. For generations,
only the rich have owned homes.
I'm studying to be *un architecto*
and hope to build homes for Mexican workers.

"My father has magical hands," he says,
brushing back a lock of his thick hair.
"He can fix almost anything. For eighteen years
he's worked in maintenance in the administrative
building at the *Instituto Politécnico Nacional,*
and still we can only rent."

"It doesn't seem right." I lace my fingers
through his as we turn a corner.

He shrugs. "My father has worked so hard
for so long, for my future."

"You must be proud of him."

In the dark, his voice warms. "I am."
He pulls me close for a kiss,
his soft lips hard against mine
as I slip my fingers through his hair.

"Puta!" comes a voice from a dark
window above the shoe shop.

Guillermo pulls away and shouts back.
"Callate! She's my girlfriend, a good woman.*"*

"I can see."

Guillermo's whole body tenses
like he's ready to scale the cement
block wall and punch the jackass.

"Please," I say to Guillermo.
"I don't want you to end up in a fight
because of his silly curses."
I keep my hand on his arm
my breath on his cheeks
          until he finally backs away.

"Both of us know the truth," I say,
"and that's all that matters."

We walk home together,
his breath ragged with rage.
When I finally stand safely
inside the Padilla's gate,
he says, *"Ten cuidado, Diana."*

"*Y tu tambien*," I raise my fingers
to my lips, kiss them, and reach
for his hand. Our fingers touch
for a few precious seconds before I back away.
          The smell of his hair lingers on my fingertips.

October 2: Phone Call

Carolina knocks on our door
around 4:30, not unexpected—
she visits us when she can,
but this time she tells me
there's a phone call for me.
"*Su novio,*" she says,
with a big smile.

I run downstairs and pick
up the phone. "*Bueno!*"

"Diana?"

"Guillermo, where are you.
It's so noisy."

"I'm on a public phone,"
he yells, "at a student meeting.
I'm so excited. I wanted to hear..."

"Is anything wrong?"
I say, barely able to hear him.

"...tu voz."

"My voice?"

"Si," he says, *"Te...."*

But there's
        a crackle
                                then another
                                                and so much static.
                        The phone line goes
                                        dead.
I hold the receiver
to my ear anyway.
Was he saying he loves me?

Finally, I put it down.
He can't reach me
if I don't hang up.
I sit on the stairs
and wait—
10 minutes
20 minutes
half an hour
an hour.

Thunder from a storm outside
rocks the building

as Natalie walks downstairs,
asks me if everything is okay.

I tell her about the call.

"Don't worry," she says.
"He probably needed to run
from the rain, and Mexican
phone service is unpredictable.
I'm sure he'll come by soon."

We climb the stairs together,
but there's still this weight,
something intangible
that I can't name,
an uneasy feeling
settling at my very core.

PART II: HISTORY LESSONS

"Our history is as rife with *caudillos* as the waters of the Gulf of Mexico are infested with sharks."

Octavio Paz
Massacre in Mexico

"...he said that it was good that God kept the truths of life from the young as they were starting out or else they'd have no heart to start at all."

Cormac McCarthy
All the Pretty Horses

The News

The next morning on the way to the bus stop,
I pass a newsstand, see the front-page story
of *The News*, a paper written in English.
It's not the stench of a drunk passed out
in a nearby alley that turns my stomach;
it's the headlines. "Troops, Snipers Clash:
22 Dead at Tlatelolco"

With clammy fingers,
I dig for *pesos* in my cloth bag
and exchange them for a paper.
I catch up with my roommates
on the university shuttle,
where others buzz with the news
that last night military surrounded
a square where students rallied.

"Around 6:00 PM snipers
from windows and rooftops
of the Tlatelolco housing project
fired on police and soldiers below."

Does Guillermo live in Tlatelolco?
Was his meeting there?

"...the gun battle lasted more than three hours."

The rattle of the bus and echo of voices
ricochet off its metal interior
as I read more.

"Hysteria broke out in the crowd
surrounded by infantrymen
and armored units."

The tanks I saw near Chapultepec Park?

"Men, women and children were trampled
as the mob fought to escape advancing troops."

I look around.
They were young people. Like us.
Herded for slaughter like penned animals.

My fingers tremble as I turn the pages
to follow the article where it continues.
"The army blames students for the shooting
and the National Defense Minister
says parents should "control their offspring,
to avoid more deaths since these benefit no one.""

How cruel to say that to their grieving parents!
They can't control their children any more
than my parents could keep me
from coming to Mexico.

I can hardly breathe,
fumble for a piece of gum,
hoping to chew away my rising nausea.
I hand off the paper to Natalie, who reads it,
pales, and passes it on to Melinda.

"This explains the phone call
I got from Javier this morning,"
Natalie says. "He hardly ever calls.
But today he said his parents were sending
him to Cuernavaca to stay with his aunt.
He won't be back until after the Olympics.
They must have sent him away to be safe."

My words rush out.
"What about Guillermo,
                              Chango?
                                        Any news?"

"No," Natalie says. "Javier didn't say much.
His parents said he had to hang up.
We were disconnected in the middle
of a sentence."

Melinda's voice sounds raspy
as she reads aloud, "Other troops advanced
with fixed bayonets and machine guns...."
She looks up and our eyes connect,
knowing this is what I described to her,
the military lines I crossed coming home
from the park. "This says J. Edgar Hoover
warned Mexico about Communist plots."

All of them, American, Russian, and Mexican,
toy with us like we're chess pieces
in a game we weren't invited to play.
First the Blacks, MLK, and the Kennedys.
Now they're coming for students.

Around us, conversations still.

I take the paper back from her and read aloud.
"Leftwing and rightwing extremists
have been promoting student demonstrations
for the past two months. At least seven were killed
and scores injured last week in gun battles
between students, police and troops after
the occupation of National University.
Troops evacuated the university
only three days ago."

I count back on my fingers.
Those were probably the troops I had crossed.
They had been marching to confront the students.
I wrap my arms tight around my body
and close my eyes. *Oh, God,*
please let Guillermo be safe.

Natalie must see my lips moving.
She scoots over to sit by me and whispers,
"I'll pray for them too."

Student Visas

As we descend steps
from the university shuttle,
people with flyers wait
outside the campus gates.

We're hesitant to take one
until we see it's a university notice;
students who have not registered
for visas must do so today, before
the influx of Olympic visitors.

Administrators will travel
with us. The bus will leave

from the statue of *Diana*
across from Chapultepec Park
at 3:00 PM.

We will need our passports,
university photo ID, and cash.
Anyone without a visa
is at risk of being sent home.

Natalie and Melinda already have visas.
I do not.

Press Release

On campus, my first stop,
as always, is the Press Room.
Whispers swirl
beneath the tap-tap-tap
of twenty-five typewriters.

Jon tells me the editor said
his wife was released
from jail without explanation.
Before they sent her away,
she saw dozens of dazed,
bloody women shoved into cells.

I ask if she finally got
medical treatment for her injuries
from the bicycle accident.

He shakes his head no
and says in a low voice,
"*Granaderos* watch admissions
at Red or Green Cross hospitals.
They'll will jail her as a student
demonstrator If she seeks help."

The faculty advisor in the Press Room
doubts official reports that only twenty
died in the sniper shootings,
says hundreds disappeared.
I lick my dry lips
and tell myself
Guillermo will call tonight.

Messages

At 3:00 I'm on the school shuttle again,
wondering if we are safe going deep
into the old city to the visa office.

My camera rests in my lap.
I want to use up the film,
have the park pictures developed
so I'll have photos of Guillermo
and can ask around about him.

Last night's storms have cleared
the air so we tug open windows.
Whenever we stop in heavy
traffic, I snap away.

Once we near the ministry,
whole streets are closed to traffic.
We wait long minutes.

As university administrators huddle,
argue in whispers,
the driver says no one will get through;
it's better to walk.

I stare out the window
at empty-faced, barefooted
children pulling shoes from crates,
lining them up. I wonder
why they don't put on a pair.
With camera clicks, I capture
the open-air market.

"Bajen aqui!" the driver demands,
as the college officials' lips tighten.
I slip my camera into my woven wool bag
and squeeze through narrow aisles to the exit.

Outside we move in a tight group
surrounded by guards; we don't stop
until we are safely inside the ministry.

I don't notice until we are walking back—
the shoes in the beggars' small hands
are stained
                    with blood.

After

My imagination must be playing tricks on me.
Surely, it's dirt or paint.
It can't be blood when there are so many shoes,
even child-sized sandals.

Stomach twisting, I turn away,
bury myself in the middle of our group
until we're inside the bus,
but then curiosity and fear take over.

Outside, armed *federales* shout
at the cowering children to cart away the shoes.
Another pulls film from a man's camera,
exposes it to the light, an ironic way to keep secrets.

Can they see me in the shadows inside the bus?
Memories from Chapultepec Park
of the tanks rolling over my flowers
assault me and I shiver.

Then some impulse, wild and raw, takes over.
I am the huntress Diana.
It's no longer about using up my film,
Click. Whirr. The film winds.

Through the fuzzy viewfinder of my Instamatic
I see work boots, canvas sneakers like Guillermo's,
women's pumps,
huaraches of every size,
all discolored and dirty. *Click. Whirr.*

Now it's about witnessing Mexican history
being erased right in front of my eyes.
I stop only when the film
fails to advance.

Back at the Padillas'

As soon as I return to our room,
I dig out my city map, study it,
locate Tlatelolco

near the ministry offices
where we were today.

My fears confirmed,
I know
yesterday
people walked in those shoes.

Silencio

I
    can't
        talk
            about
                the
                    shoes.
When my roommates come back
from seeing a movie, an American comedy,
they find me crying in a corner of the balcony.

Melinda and Natalie think I'm suffering
from a broken heart;
I can't argue with that.

I sit in our room,
journal open in my lap,
staring at empty pages.

Neither Guillermo nor Chango call.
Natalie thinks they may be visiting family
like Javier, although silly Melinda
tells herself Chango hasn't called
because she finally kissed him.

She says, "Either I'm the world's worst kisser
or Chango is afraid I only kissed him
because I think we're engaged."
Melinda lives in her own little world,
but she doesn't need to know my fears.
Her suffering wouldn't change anything.

I have nightmares,
spend hours wandering with spirits
searching for Guillermo's sneakers.

He would call if he could
so he must be in prison, injured,
or dead. I can feel it.

And there's nothing I can do.
My grief is a mute animal
clawing at my insides
and the pain never stops.

Breakdown

The next day as Natalie and I
walk to the university shuttle,
a woman with swollen pouches
beneath her empty eyes passes us.
Tears have streaked her lined cheeks.

For all I know, she could
have lost someone at *Tlatelolco*.
She could even be Guillermo's
mother, wondering where her son is.
I lean against the side of a soot-
stained building and cross my arms
over my aching insides.

Natalie stops, waits for me
to catch my breath so I can speak.

My jagged words tear through the exhaust-
filled air as I reveal what I witnessed
from the bus. "I don't understand," I say.
"Where are the families of all the people
who disappeared? Why don't they
speak up?"

Natalie puts a soft hand on my arm.
"I'll ask Javier when he gets back.
Maybe he can tell us how to find Guillermo."

Her words feel like salt
                    on a scraped knee, but worse.

"Your boyfriend is safe,"
I snap. "I can't wait."

Her face reddens but she stays with me.

I walk to the curb
and raise my arm to hail a taxi.
"I'll go to every hospital and jail and morgue,"
I say in a choked voice, "until I find him."

Far stronger than I expect,
Natalie grabs my arm, twists it
behind my back and shoves me
away from the *Reforma*.
"Are you insane? It's too risky."

"Wait," Natalie continues.
"Just wait until tonight.
I'll take Melinda to the movies
and you can talk to Carolina alone
when she comes upstairs. Ask her.
The maids know about everything
that happens in the city."

I try to wrench my arm away
but that girl has the strength
of an Amazon.

"Think," she says. "Just take
a few deep breaths and think.
You know I'm right."
Then she drops my arm.

I pivot, ready to tell her she's an idiot,
but she slips right past me and heads
for the university shuttle.

I stand there, sides heaving,
gasping for air, hating her
for being right.

That Night

When Carolina comes
upstairs to turn down our beds,
I grip my journal in both hands
and tell her I haven't seen or spoken
to Guillermo since Tlatelolco.

Deep lines form between her eyebrows
as she draws them together.

I invite her to sit down,
but she won't, always stands.

I ask her why people don't talk
about the missing, search
harder for loved ones.

"No pueden." They can't.
Carolina says her *novio's* uncle
went to *Lecumberri* prison
looking for his son.
He had to sign in,
give personal information.

The *policia* tracked him from that list
and threatened his family.
People who ask questions
are accused of crimes, arrested.
Others lose their jobs.
They are afraid.
"Nunca haces preguntas.
Never ask questions.
Es muy peligroso," she says,
as her eyes fill with tears.
"Lo siento." I'm sorry.
Without another word
she slips out the door into the night.

With trembling hands
I shut my journal, consider
the safest place to hide it.

Exodus

Natalie convinces Melinda and me
to follow Javier's lead
and leave the city, at least
for the first week of the Olympics.
We decide on a low-cost university-sponsored trip
to *Guanajuato* and *San Miguel de Allende.*

The school must want us out of the city too,
to offer tours at such bargain rates.

Before we go, I lock my film and journal
inside the case of my useless electric typewriter,
hide it in the back of our stuffed closet.

I haven't admitted to my parents yet—
the typewriter isn't compatible
with Mexico's electrical current.
Kind of like me.

Packing My Shoes

I fight nausea,
stick to sandals
until I imagine
my painted toenails
drenched in
Guillermo's
blood,
run into
the bathroom
to vomit.

Escape

The bus takes us northwest
through the rugged countryside.
I feel my fears retreat
with each passing kilometer,
feel safe for the first time in days.

We enter an older, quieter world,
one with *paisanos* leading *burros*
up rocky green mountain paths.
Guanajuato is in a valley, a village

maze of narrow, winding streets,
surrounded by buildings of sage
green, sienna, lemon adobe.

The local university, as well
as the *Basilica* and *Teatro Juarez*,
sleep in the noon sun, as if to say
what Guillermo said to me in the park,
"No te preocupes. Todo esta bien."
Don't worry. Everything is okay.

I breathe, push my worries away,
try to believe Guillermo has survived,
will call me, somehow, someday,
which works until we wander
through *el Callejon del Beso,*
Alley of the Kiss, so narrow lovers
can kiss from opposite balconies
while strolling musicians serenade.

I met Guillermo only weeks ago,
so why am I now filled
with a loss beyond tears,
a heart torn in two?

Refuge

Everything is a work of art
        in San Miguel de Allende.
A rainbow of parrots squawk
        in the garden outside our room.
Scarlet poinsettias frame *Los Monjas,*
        a distant domed church.
Fuchsia flowers spill
        from our tiled roof.
A rope and plank swing dangles
        from a stout-trunked tree.
A small boy in his underwear
        eats *jicama* on dusty steps
        in front of a rough hewn door.

Their beauty scrapes against me,
        sandpaper,
as I wait for the flip side in what I know now
        is a fallen Garden of Eden,
        my Mexico.

Power Outage

Nothing is visible—
        no pinprick of light anywhere,
our room blacker than the inside of a coffin.

When we pull back the curtain,
        it is the same.
The mountains and lush foliage
        block all light from moon and stars.
We fumble our way to our purses,
        bumping into each other in the dark.
But we are not smokers, have no lighters
        or flashlights or candles
and don't dare open the door,
        night a perfect cover
        for animals on the hunt.

The Dark Side

Smothered by thick darkness,
I try not to panic as night
wraps me up tighter and tighter
and I struggle to breathe.
I wish Guillermo were here,
his strong arms around me.

Unlike the parrots, now quiet,
we talk to survive the night,
but my lips are tight with tension
as I battle angry thoughts.

I did not sign up for this.
The glossy brochure—

Build your Future at
Accredited American College in Mexico!
        did
                not
                        say
Olympic dreams of peace
are just another Mexican myth,

Strangers I meet in public places
may be Communist instigators,

Tanks and bayonet toting troops
may block my way home,

Fearful citizens don't report
human slaughter in the streets.

Natalie and Melinda talk themselves to sleep.
By morning a power outage won't matter.
We can move on, buy flashlights, candles, matches.

But I am stuck
sleepless and struggling,
wondering how I can go on,
if Mexico has killed Guillermo
and defeated me.

My Picks for Seven Deadly Sins

I create a new list,
the deadliest,
for my time in Mexico,
a *piñata* with seven cones of evil:

Blind obedience
Greed
Deceit
Absence of Empathy
Hatred
Preoccupation with Public Perception
Murder

I Remember Another Sleepless Night

Grandpa died two weeks
before my fifteenth birthday.
After the funeral, not knowing
what to do, I stood alone in the kitchen
for hours, rubbing a faded dishrag
across the soapy sides of lipstick-
stained china teacups,
anxious when I discovered
cracks in the porcelain.

Spilled water dampened the belly
of my A-line dress, spotted
the green linoleum floor,
but still I washed, rinsed,
set saucers in rows
along the drying rack.

Mother pushed open the swinging
door from the dining room
and joined me at the sink,
long enough to ask me to spend the night
with my grieving grandmother
who might not allow her to stay,
but wouldn't refuse a granddaughter's offer.

I twisted the rag so tight I could see blue
rivers of veins on the pale backs of my hands;
I couldn't say no to my fatherless mother.

Grandma fell asleep fast, while I lay next to her,
where Grandpa had slept only days before.
He was a watchmaker.
Clocks all over the apartment
chimed the quarter hour
all night long, an eternity,
a fraction of the infinite time
I would have to live without him.

I Don't Wake My Roommates

but I pace at the foot of our beds—
five steps, turn, five steps, turn.

While I walk, I plan.

Tonight I have to believe
Guillermo is alive, out there
somewhere. Tonight.

Tomorrow I'll buy flashlights
and batteries to carry in my purse...
always. Tomorrow.

Next week I'll find a safe lab,
find a safe lab to develop my film.
I've waited long enough. Next week.

I pretend I'm in control,
even when I'm not.

Silence Echoes

more than
            screams from a mountain top,
                        clanging garbage can lids at
5:00 a.m. after a night of drinking,
            or gunshots in a city canyon.

Silence ricochets
            off walls in empty rooms,
                        reverberates, suffocates,
                        speaks with more finality than a
cement lid over a lowered coffin.

Silence always has the final word.

Morning Comes

As onyx skies fade to gray,
exhausted, I sleep. Later,
when Melinda opens the curtains,
I awaken to filtered sunlight.

She dances through the dust moats.
"I can see! I can see!" she sings.
"And today we'll buy flashlights."

Natalie and I chorus the hallelujahs.

Emotional Olympics

After we return to the city,
my feelings flip back-and-forth
like *papel picado,* the paper cut-outs
dangling overhead in fan-cooled cafes.

I fell in love with Guillermo
and the country at the same time
so I want to hate it
the way mourners hate the sun
for warming their shattered world.

But Mexico mesmerizes me again,
its beauty spins colors:
from *pasteles* to *rebozos,*
Siquiero's frescos to dahlia bouquets,
an eternal spring impossible to resist,
but full of memories of Guillermo.

Melinda and I go to the Olympics—
Women's Volleyball, Japan versus Poland.
The women on the Polish team are huge,
remind me of the towering players
that terrified me in high school PE classes,
but the lithe Japanese pound them
3-0 for the win. The crowd roars
its approval, and so do we.

But later, as we walk away from the games,
a stranger grabs my groin and disappears
before I can even see him, much less
process how violated I feel.

In a flash, I'm furious and fearful
again, reminded of the dark underbelly
of Mexico, an exotic animal
laying in wait to tear away flesh.

Basilica

We make the most of the remaining
days of the Olympic Break by visiting
"safe" tourist destinations. *The Basilica,*

Our Lady of Guadalupe, tops our list.
Surely there, God will protect us.

Outside on the plaza we listen
to our tour guide as heat and people
press around us from all sides.
He says that in 1531 the Virgin Mary
appeared to a native peasant *Juan Diego
Cuauhtlatoatzin* and asked him to tell the bishop
she wanted a temple built in her honor.

After the bishop demanded proof, Juan Diego
went back to *Tepeyac* hill to find her.
Mary emerged as the Virgin of Guadalupe.
She told him to pick roses and carry them
back to the bishop in his *tilma*, his wrap.

When Juan Diego returned and opened
his cloak, the roses fell at their feet,
and the image of the Virgin miraculously
appeared inside the *tilma*, which now hangs
on the walls of her cathedral.

What a great story! I shift from foot to foot
anxious to see this relic that has survived hundreds
of years, even after 1921, when a man planted
and detonated a bomb hidden in a flower vase.
It severely damaged the building,
but the *tilma* survived intact.

Inside the basilica, we're surrounded by the scent
of incense, lit candles, and lemon oil used
to polish the wood. We sit on the pews
and study the Virgin, serene in the cloak,
dark cyan trimmed in gold. To me
          she looks like any other lovely work of art,
an image painted on canvas cloth,
a miracle created by an artist,
not The Artist.

My heart registers nothing but loss.

My Father's Daughter

I lean back and look up
at the soaring Doric columns
that support a domed ceiling covered in gold.

My father works for store crafters who design
and build all kinds of interiors. He'd appreciate
the workmanship, especially since his company
once covered a department store's walls in gold leaf.

If he saw these ornate walls, though,
I think his eyes would fill with tears
not because of the beauty,
and it *is* beautiful,
but because of all the pilgrims outside,
rough stones tearing at their knees
as they crawl across the plaza to the church,
to beg the Virgin for mercy or healing
or a miracle equal to Juan Diego's.
I wonder if Guillermo's mother is
one of them.

At the end of the tour, the guide reveals
the Shrine of Guadalupe is endangered.
Built on a lake in earthquake prone Mexico City,
its foundation is unstable and sinking;
the earth underfoot threatens
all who live, visit, and pray here.

Finally Javier...

comes back from visiting
his *abuelos* in a small *pueblo*.
I corner him, ask if he's heard
from Guillermo or Chango
since the student massacre.

He says I must have misunderstood—
the language difference—
there was no massacre.
His father told him a few troublemakers
were contained before the Olympics,
but nothing to worry about;
our friends wouldn't have been there
            because they're gentlemen.

95

He insists:
Chango never would have gone
to an evening demonstration.
He drives his grandmother to six o'clock mass,
and it's her VW so he can't say no.

"Guillermo?" I ask again.

He shrugs. "I haven't seen him.
But don't worry.
He's probably busy."
Javier says he'll introduce me to other friends...

like men are interchangeable,
like Guillermo is disposable,
doesn't matter, or possibly even exist.

Natalie can read my rising anger.
She knows I want to slap him. Hard.
"Time to go, Javier," she says, taking
his hand and dragging him to the door
while mouthing, "I'm sorry."

"No, wait," I hiss. "Just one more question.
Javier, does your father
work for the government?"

His ridged forehead thickens as he frowns
and he squints at me when he asks,
"Yes. How did you know?"

My head drops as they walk out the door.
No wonder his father sent Javier away so quickly.
He probably had inside information,
a lot more than he shared with his student son.

Melinda "Comforts" Me

"Mexican men," she sputters.
"What is wrong with them?
How could Javier say that to you?
He doesn't have a clue about how we feel.

"I shouldn't be surprised. The guys here
don't even bother to make dates with us.
          They expect us to wait around for them,

96

like we have nothing better to do.

"And Chango! If he didn't want me
to kiss him back, why did he keep
trying to kiss me, and once I did,
why did he disappear?

"Not to mention the whole city lights fiasco.
And how men stalk us and catcall on the streets.
No respect.

"Who knows why Guillermo hasn't shown up?
No point in thinking the worst. He's probably fine,
just doing his macho Mexican guy thing.

"I have an idea," she says. "Let's only date
Americans while we're here."

As usual, Melinda's "logic" leaves me
bewildered and speechless.

Tinder

I'm so angry with Javier
that I can't look at him,
never speak to him,
rarely speak to Natalie,
and when I do, I'm snippy.

I know I'm not being fair,
but her boyfriend isn't missing,
He's here, alive, with her.

Not acknowledging the massacre
doesn't change the fact

that Tlatelolco happened
and not hearing from Guillermo
is   a   very   big   deal.

It never ends, my wondering
if he's rotting in a mass grave
or beaten bloody and lying naked
in his own urine at *Lecumberri* prison,
El Palacio de la Maldad.

My anger mounts at everyone,
even Guillermo

for putting himself in danger
and disappearing from my life.

Could I have kept him safe?
Is his disappearance my fault?
I carry all this tinder inside,
not knowing when it will next spark.

Distracted I walk past the shoe repair.
The owner, as usual,
runs out and screams,
"Puta!"

I cross the street,
turn at a safe distance
to study his anger-mottled face,
wonder who left him,
what fuels his fury
toward a young woman
he doesn't even know.

Passing the Flower Cart

Their smell pierces the air.
I start crying
and can't stop.
The smell of roses
will forever haunt me.

Natalie Sounds Off

Natalie stands at the end of my bed
and chews me out. "You say I shouldn't
hang around hoping Javier will show up
when all of Mexico City lies outside our windows,
but you are the biggest hypocrite ever
because that's exactly what you've been doing
for weeks. You moon around, writing
                    in your journal, pretending to study,

"waiting for Guillermo to call

98

when you barely knew him.

"You're so convinced he's dead,
but he could be anywhere.
Maybe his parents sent him away,
maybe he had to get a job,
maybe he fell for someone else.
Are you going to lie around here
forever and miss all the fun?

"Javier brought two of his friends
and we're going to take a ride
through Las Lomas. Melinda is coming
with us, and if you have half a brain,
you will too. So brush your hair,
put on some lipstick, come downstairs,
and smile. With you or without you,
we're leaving in ten minutes."

Trying to Move On

My head tells me Natalie is right
so I try. I go downstairs.
Everyone welcomes me
as if I haven't been
a moody bitch for weeks.
           Javier's friend Luis surprises me too.
           He's tall, wears wire-rimmed John Lennon
           glasses over his gray eyes.
           He has a sandy brown mustache
           and carries a camera with him
           everywhere, like me.
Oscar is a round, loveable
Sancho Panza with thick fingers
           and a constant smile.
           Impossible not to like him.
We pack into the car,
three across on bench seats
in an old jalopy.
Luis drives with petite
Melinda sandwiched
between him and Oscar.
           I'm in the back with Javier
           and Natalie, trying hard
           to focus on speaking Spanish.
           Unfortunately, I still don't have

a good grasp of idioms
because I say something
that sets the guys off laughing.
My request for a common translation
leaves them blushing and silent.
I'm embarrassed for even longer.

Day of the Dead

We wander streets of psychedelic dreams.
From the smudged November night,
incense and candlelight, a rosy pink glow
rises from graves and halos stooped women.

Against the chill, they wrap themselves
tight in smoky wool *rebozos*.
Families feast on favorite foods
of deceased relatives buried
beneath their picnics in graveyards.
Life and death go hand-in-hand like lovers.

Luminous white skeletons,
loose bones clacking,
dance through cobbled streets
where ancient stone spires point
to the scurry of murky clouds.

Church bells toll, summon spirits.
Ghouls offer sugared skulls,
place marigolds on family altars,
believing that souls of ancestors
celebrate with them on this day.

Families of the missing, silenced,
lost like me in the dense dark,
conceal leaden hearts, swallow unshed tears,
pray for knowledge, closure, sunrise.

Mail Call

Letters for us, left on the Padillas'
telephone table, never gather dust.
Usually Melinda gets to them first,
climbs the flights of stairs as easily
as a child scrambling up a jungle gym.

She tosses envelopes on our beds
before settling in to read hers.

I watch Melinda's eyes scan each line.
Sometimes they fill with tears;
more often her skin wrinkles
into a smile. She never reveals
any of the contents of those letters.

Curiosity wins.
I walk over and sit on her bed.
She immediately folds up the letter
and fans herself with it.

"That envelope smells good, Melinda.
Is that men's cologne? English Leather?"

She blushes and nods.

"Guy back home?"

"Uh-huh."

"He sure writes you a lot.
I recognize those envelopes."

She nods and bites her lip
like she is trying not to cry.

"And?"

She puts down the letter and fidgets
with her belt. "Well, we were kind of
going steady last year."

Now we were getting somewhere.

"Oh, so you miss him."
It shouldn't surprise me
that flirty Melinda left a broken-hearted
boyfriend in Louisiana.
But this feels different;
she's more serious,
like she really cares about this guy.

"Is he why you're here?
Do your parents not like him?"

Melinda rears back
like I have offended her.
"Of course not.
Lonnie is a great guy."

She takes a breath.
"But my parents married at eighteen.
They want me to get a degree
and what they call 'life experience.'
I don't know why that's such a big deal.
They've done okay without degrees."

Her parents' wishes make sense to me,
but I know from her "sad dog"
expression that I better not say that.
I give her a hug.

She kisses the envelope
and puts it under her pillow.

I walk back to my bed, lie down,
and close my stinging eyes.
Missing Guillermo is a jagged rock
that slices me open at unexpected times.

My problem isn't being homesick for people
                                    who write;
it's waiting for the letter that never comes,
                        the one telling me he's okay.
Every day I check the mail and the obituaries.
                Every day there's nothing.
An invisible hand has totally erased him.

Letter from Mother

She writes me weekly,
when she's under the dryer
at the beauty salon.

"Tomorrow is the election.
Stop worrying about Nixon.
I have an idea he'll continue
                Johnson's programs—I hope
he can accomplish so much
good he'll be re-elected.
How about Muskie-Kennedy
                        in '76?"

What Mother Doesn't Know

I wish I could vote.
Humphrey/Muskie are ho-hum,
but Nixon/Agnew scare me,
the way they divide people,
the whole students versus establishment
mind-set at home and here in Mexico,
"Us" versus "Them" is what
I've learned to fear.

Inquiring Reporter

True to his word, Javier brings over lots
of guys to meet Melinda and me.
Apparently American girls are very popular,
maybe because we appear freer in every way.
Do they hope we will be fun flings?

In whispered conversations, I've heard
about married Mexican men
and their *"casas chicas,"*
the mistresses they set up in separate households.
Ugh. Back to the virgins and the whores.

Even those young wives
I met in the steam room
were like "kept" women,
their only mission in life
to please their husbands.
I've never wanted to be either
married or mistress.

There's a whole world
out there to discover.
Why would I want to trade that
for four walls, furniture,
and flowers to arrange?

Many of the Javier's friends speak little English
so communication is always a challenge,
but one night I decide to use Diana the Huntress
skills to find answers to my questions.

I challenge Javier in front of his friends,
all known by first name or nickname only.

They could be made up for all I know.
"What was Guillermo's whole name?" I ask.
"His real name. I never knew it."

He ignores my use of past tense.
With his arm tightening
around Natalie's shoulders,
he answers in present,
"Guillermo Cordero del Rey."

I turn to the new boys.
"Have you seen him?"
No one admits to seeing him
or even ever knowing him.
They laugh and say it's a big city;
there are too many *Guillermos* to count.

My fear is that there is one less
and that I'll never know it.

Tomorrow.
Tomorrow I'll ask the Press Room
photographer to develop my film,

our snapshots together. Afraid to face
the possible truth, I've waited long enough.

With a name and our park photos,
 maybe then I can bribe someone
 to find out what happened. But
our pictures in the park

and the shots of the shoes
were on the same roll.
I'll have to find someone
I can trust.

Dark Room

The next day I pace outside
as a red light blinks over the door,
warning that exposure to any light
at this stage in the process
could destroy the film.

After other writers send curious
glances in my direction,
I know I have to stop—
it's dangerous to call attention
to the photos. I say a silent prayer
that the developer's curiosity
isn't aroused by the shoe shots.

I try to distract the rest of the staff.
"On a deadline," I say. "Inquiring Reporter."
Like that is urgent, late-breaking news.
They laugh—most consider me a pet,
the Press Room mascot—
too young and green to threaten,
but dependable for copy.

I force myself to sit down and type,
"What Would You Change?"
an article asking campus students
about how to improve the university.

Some suggest silly things—
a swimming pool stocked with fish,
or the university relocating to Acapulco
so students can surf,
but the serious asked for better resources,
like a quieter, more efficient library.

If anyone asked me, I'd say we need
to track students so someone would know
if we're carted away in the dead of night.

I leave my text in the editor's box
and wander around the corner again.
The light is off! My hands are clammy.
Am I ready to see the photos?
Will I ever be?

The photographer Jon comes out,
his pale eyebrows lifted in a question.
"What's with all the shoes?
Do you have a muddy shoe fetish?"

Even though I used black and white
film and he can't see the bloodstains,
he knows something is off.

Can I trust him
or is he going to put us both at risk
by talking about what he's seen?
Will he connect them to the massacre?

Under the weight of my thick hair,
sweat collects on my neck.
I swallow, try to calm my heaving
stomach. "Just trying to use up film.
I took these near a construction site."

He studied one. "Some of these shoes
are awfully small for construction workers."

I shrug and force out my words
through tense lips. "There's a tiny maid
in our house that's barely a teenager.
People go to work young here."

"Whatever you say," he says,
looking me over from head to toe.
I reach for the prints, but he lifts them
high, out of my reach.
Is he interested in me or
does he know something's up?

"So you have a boyfriend?" he asks.

It feels like a kick in the gut.
How do I answer that?
I have to say something
or he'll never give me the pictures.

"Maybe," I say, tipping my head,
and doing a sorry imitation
of Melinda flirting. I put my hand
on his arm. "And maybe not."

Somehow I manage a vertical leap,
and snatch the photos out of his hand.
The faculty advisor comes in then,
gives us a sharp look.

"Our inquiring reporter is in a hurry,"
Jon says in his Georgia drawl. He turns
to leave, blocking our advisor's view
with his back and whispers,
"Meet me in the cafeteria:
I'll reveal the secrets of the darkroom."

What does he mean?
That he knows I have secrets too?
Did the shoe shots indicate a date
or did he recognize the location
as being close to the student slaughter?

I'm not sure I can trust him.
He could share the photos with others
so I have no choice about meeting him,
if only to be sure he doesn't tell anyone.

I think of the police ripping rolls of film
from the cameras of unsuspecting photographers
and I don't know how to protect Jon.
Lifting my heavy book bag, I pull it
over my shoulder, the weight of my books
far lighter than the worries I carry inside.

What I See

I can't risk others from the press seeing my photos
so I leave and find an empty bench under a tree.
Counting them first, I pray all the photos
and negatives are there, that Jon has not kept any.
When numbers match, I take a deep breath.

The shoe pictures are on top.
Somehow they aren't as scary in black
and white, but there are so many—
huaraches, dress leather, Converse sneakers.

They range from child-sized to man-sized.
Clearly more than 22 died at *Tlatelolco*
and they weren't all college students.
            I wonder again why there isn't an outcry
            from victims' families, but then I think
            of Guillermo's father, a maintenance worker
            at Mexico's national university,
            still surrounded by armed guards.
 All the times I've wanted to talk with Sr. Cordero,
I've stopped myself, remembered
he needs to protect his wife and daughters.
Maybe it takes silence for them to survive.
Maybe everyone has something to fear.
I look at the photos in my lap,
thumb through them until I come
to the one of Guillermo and me.
We are looking at each other, eyes locked,
like we can't possibly look away,
not even for the few seconds needed
to snap a picture.
            It's not only the sun that lights our faces.
            He looks like someone in love,
            not someone who would stay away.
And before his "student meeting,"
he called. What had he said
when the phone disconnected?
Te...amo? That he loved me?

Unexpected Comfort

I hate to cry in public, but I can't stop.
With my hands covering my face, I sob.
Then I feel someone sit next to me.

Once I catch my breath,
I open my eyes and see a woman
in a plaid skirt and white blouse,
regular street clothes, except
she wears a nun's black head covering.
Looking off in the distance, she waits
for me to calm myself, then digs
in her pocket and hands me tissues.

"Thank you."
I wipe my eyes and nose.

She smiles and says in English,
"I'm Sister Cecilia.
Is there anything I can do to help?"

Her quiet kindness sets me off again.
"I wish you could help," I sob,
"but I don't think anyone can."
When I look up again,
I see her studying me.
She has a compassionate face.
White wisps of hair sneak out
from her black scarf
and frame her blue eyes.
        I pause, look into her kind eyes,
        and tell her everything...
        about the phone call and my fears
        that the troops I saw killed Guillermo.
She nods and listens.
"Nice looking young man,"
she says when I show her his picture.
"I understand why you're worried.
 Do you know his family
or their parish name?"

I shake my head.
"All I know is his name:
Guillermo Cordero del Rey."

"Are you pregnant?"

I stiffen "No!"

"You're sure?"

"I'm not the Virgin Mary,"
I snap, and instantly feel guilty.
"Sorry," I say. "I meant to say
it's not possible." Somehow,
I don't seem to have offended her.

She continues in her soft voice.
"I can see why you're upset, especially
since there is nothing you can do
or even should do as an American student."

Those words bring surprising comfort.
Her listening and simple acknowledgment
that my anxiety is understandable helps.

"I'll be on the lookout for any information
about Guillermo. May I have your name
so I can contact you if I hear anything?"

"Diana. Diana Greene. Thank you."

She stands up and smoothes her plaid skirt.
"I'm sure I'll see you around campus,
Diana. And I'll be praying for both of you."

"Thank you, but I'm not Catholic," I say.
"I'm Jewish."

She laughs, "We pray for everyone."

Uh-Oh

I forget to meet Jon for lunch.
Bad move when I need him
to keep my secrets.

I finally find him on the grassy rise
outside the post office.
        I feel guilty for exposing him
to those photos, like I owe him
something for developing the film.
        I apologize for missing lunch,

110

and he asks if I want to see
where he's crashing in a school.

I hesitate.

Jon's cute in an Anglo way—
washed denim blue eyes
shoulder-length blonde hair,
fair skin, a true *gringo*.
He's seen my photos,
knows I have (had?) a *novio*.
And Melinda would approve
because he's American.
I feel an unexpected flash of anger
toward Guillermo for not being here.
I owe him nothing.

Why not see Jon's place?
So I climb into his brown van
and we head down the two-lane
mountain road to the city,
Jon's speech is slow, disjointed
as we weave in and out of traffic,
the buses belching diesel, taxis honking.

Is he stoned?

Those campy high school movies
like Reefer Madness
about marijuana causing insanity
and God-knows-what-else,
I never believed them,
but, after years of hearing my cigarette
addicted dad hack up his lungs,
I've never wanted to smoke...anything.

Is Jon safe to drive?

He parks along a busy avenue
and disappears around back. Minutes later
he opens the deserted building from the inside.
It's pretty—red tile floors, frosted glass windows,
but very little furniture. Jon camps out
on a Mexican blanket that covers the bare floor.
He rolls a joint, offers me a toke,
talks about harvesting weed at night
                    in the garden surrounding the playground.

I'm relieved Jon hasn't flirted with me
since we left the Press Room, especially
because I don't see anything lying around
that suggests he has roommates.

Is he squatting here?
Do I need to worry about *policia*?

I can imagine the newspaper article—
American Students Hiding
in Abandoned School—
another excuse to beat us, jail us
or make us disappear forever.
My parents, who trust me, would never
find me. It would kill them.

Maybe Jon is only a lost, lonely guy,
looking for someone to join him in a high,
but the distance between us
is as insurmountable as the distant volcanoes.
I can't help him with his demons
and he can't help me with mine.
We're a sad pair, but now I know his secrets too.
I ask him to never tell anyone about my photos,
say that my parents don't know about my *novio*.

He nods dreamily and stretches out on the blanket.
I don't want to lie down next to him
or get back in the van with him,
so I make an excuse about a test tomorrow,
that I want to shop on my way home.

He's chill with that so I let myself out,
hoping if I follow *Mariano Escobedo*,
the main street where we parked,
I'll find my way home.

But when I emerge from the overgrown bushes
that conceal the school
and walk on the teeming sidewalks
with the growl of passing buses,
staccato of people bargaining with street vendors,
waves of dizziness overcome me.

Vertigo

Some people like spinning
                            the giddy rotation

things randomly appearing,

        disappearing from the periphery

a slow motion out-of-control
                            inability   to focus

                                        tasted
    in tea cup rides
                    wine glasses
                            tokes

contact highs

                            pill bottles.

        But close your eyes
                        for even a moment
and the dizzy darkness
                                        sucks you in
                    circling in-and-out

        a sickening spin

lifting yourself up
                        challenging as
                            climbing Himalayas.

    The trick is to keep moving
                        run a hand along a brick wall

cling to the sticky metal railing

            teeter on the stained

curb
                grab a lamp pole

                                        until it passes

keep moving
                        no matter

        what.

113

Sister Cecilia

expresses delight
that I want to write
about her first ecumenical meeting,
her promise to promote
connections among students.

At the event, the words of "Amazing Grace"
swell around us. "I once was lost,
but now I'm found..."
I need that reassurance
that we are not alone,
faith that my classmates
and I won't vanish like Guillermo,
I sing too loud, "...was blind, but now I see."

Eventually "Let There Be Peace on Earth"
and "Michael Rowed the Boat Ashore"
become "The Eternal Gifts of Christ the King"
while I shift my weight from leg to leg,
clasp my sweaty hands. The gathering turns
into a Christian worship service. I worry now
that we're about to kneel,
something Jews don't do.

Like any good journalist,
I report on the gathering
                          objectively,
but later I talk to Sister Cecilia,
say non-denominational Christian
isn't Interfaith, can't serve the needs
of *all* students in an international city
where people disappear overnight.

She understands
that I won't join her group,
but she doesn't change her mission.
Those vows she took long ago
                          stuck.

Cruel

When I read Mother's letter,
        warning me to stay away from Jon,
        not to associate with anyone using pot
        because Mexican laws are even harsher
        than ones in the U.S."
I ask myself why I told her about him,
        and the answer surprises me.

I want my parents to worry about me
        because they never have,
to know they can no longer
        make decisions for me,
to realize how important I am
        to them,
and, for once, to focus on middle kid
        me.

I shared my Jon story to be mean.

But I don't tell them everything.
        I don't tell them about Guillermo.

Everything they know of Tlatelolco
        is what they have read in U.S. newspapers,
        next to nothing,
and I reassure them I am far
        away from that area of the city.

Running through the armed soldiers,
        the power outage in San Miguel—
all are top secret so they don't insist
        I return home.
Puta Man? I'll never tell them.

What's truly painful,
the greater dangers,
I keep to myself
so they won't worry.
Maybe I'm only cruel
some of the time.

Another Broken Wing

One spring-like fall afternoon,
when we get back from school,
the house is in an uproar.

Sra. Padilla has been hurt
in a car accident. We try to find
which hospital she's in, but it's tricky
because the Mexican Red
and Green Cross emergency services
fight over the injured.

As dinner goes uneaten,
we discover Sra. Padilla,
like my editor's wife,
has been detained at a police station
and hasn't received medical care.
We call for a cab and go check on her.

With sweaty hands, I smooth down my skirt,
an attempt to make it longer, lower my eyes
as we cross cracked stones at the entrance.
If only I could forget horror stories
of people never returning from encounters
with Mexican law enforcement.

Sra. Padilla's ever-present pearl
necklace and earrings are gone,
I hope not lost to bribes.
Scarlet spots stand out
in relief on her pale cheeks,
almost like she's wearing white face.

Señora holds her right arm close
to her body. My stomach twists
when *Señor* says she has broken
her collar bone, but the police
have not yet released her
to her doctor.

The Padillas are touched to see us
there, but they reassure us
and firmly send us back to their house.

The next morning we learn
they arrived home after 3:00 AM.
The *Señora* has a white cast
covering the top half of her body.
Doctors have set her right arm
in an upright position,
like she's hailing a taxi.

Natalie, Melinda, and I don't speak
at breakfast, try not to disturb them.
Their bedroom door, always open
at meal times, is closed today.

I want to do the same;
close a door on pain,
huddle in a dark room.
So many fault lines run
through Mexico City.
I, too, tremble.

Mountain Trail

One Saturday, we go horseback riding.
Luis's jalopy wheezes through the hairpin turns
as we drive up into the mountains.

At one of many meadows
we bump down a gravel path to park
and tumble out of the car onto a grassy rise.
We are the only ones here. There's no stable
or track or sign of horses anywhere.

"Are you sure this is the right place?"

"I'm sure." Oscar beams with excitement.

As if on cue, we see some *paisanos* leading horses
over a ridge. I have no idea how they knew
we were here. The men, so much smaller
than the horses, jog toward us, holding the reins
loosely in their hands. The animals are huge;
I'm only as tall as their saddles.

"Luis," I say, "Did I tell you
I've never been on a horse?"

"Yes. None of us knows how to ride either."

"That doesn't make me feel any better.
At least Natalie knows what's she's doing."
The altitude up here is around 9,000 feet
so I don't know whether it's fear
or thin air that makes me feel light-headed.

Of course the men help Melinda mount
the smallest horse. She's up, laughing
and bouncing through the meadow first.

Oscar climbs onto a horse which is short and sturdy
like he is. Ever the jolly gentleman, he follows her,
his thick legs dangling. He looks like the drawing of *Sancho
        Panza* in my *Don Quixote* text.
I laugh as the local men lead them away.

Natalie scales her horse with ease
and talks Javier through the steps
before they head out, which leaves
Luis and me.

"Sure is big," I say as I face the shiny
flank of the monster. A small *paisano*
tries to lift me, a total embarrassment,
so I suck up my courage and wave him away.

I stand with my shoulder to the horse's flank,
facing the hind end like Natalie did.
Then I grip the saddle horn
with both sweaty hands and pull myself up
until I can get my left foot set in the stirrup.
Then I can swing my right leg around.
The way I am grunting and sweating,
I sound like a 300 pound man
instead of a 115 pound girl.

Luis, who has a height advantage,
has no trouble mounting the horse,
but his posture is stiff
and he grips the reins
like a mountain climber grips a rope.
Maybe he's terrified too.
I laugh at him, he laughs at me,
but we are up and moving.
In the moments when I'm not terrified,
I love the view from up here.

Except for Natalie,
whose trainer leaves the reins to her alone,
the other men jog next to us,
probably to protect the horses.

With all the wide open spaces, the language
barrier, and our lack of knowledge,
the horses go wherever they want,
which works just fine until I decide to catch up
with Luis, his fine hair bouncing as he rides.
I clap my feet against my horse's flanks,
like the cowboys do on television.

My horse takes off, leaving the *paisanos*
far behind, while I slip over to the left,
barely hanging on as we rocket past Luis.

Looking over my shoulder to call for help,
I slide down farther, my body now halfway down
the beast's side, which my horse does not
                                    appreciate.
He jerks and twists as if he'll toss me at any second.

My life doesn't flash before my eyes.
        My fears do.
I don't want to be trampled by a horse
        on a remote mountain in Mexico,
the Red and Green Cross arguing
        over my broken body,
taking me to a police station
        where someone will need to pay off
officials before I can go to a hospital.
        "Help!" I scream. "*Ayudame!*"

That's when something very strange happens.
I feel Guillermo presence. He says,
        "You've got this, *chica*."
And, somehow, I believe him.

I grip the saddle horn and, inch by sweaty inch,
        pull myself up.
When I'm finally upright, I grab the reins
        with one hand and tug on them
until the snorting horse slows,
        tossing his head as if he's asking,

"What took you so long?"

With the others far behind, I draw
        the reins to the right until we circle back
the way we came, moving at a slow,
        steady pace. I take a deep breath
and finally relax into the ride.

Maybe all that romantic stuff in books
        and movies is all wrong.
Maybe *being* loved isn't a magical charm
        that saves us from a terrible fate.
Maybe *our* loving someone,
        knowing what they'd want for us,
simply helps us become braver, stronger.

Seesaw

If only I had told Guillermo about the troops,
or warned him to stay off the streets,
then he'd be here.

Or if I had asked more about his family,
I would know how to contact them.
But I had been too self-centered to do either.

Each time I ask Javier if he has seen him,
he says no, that Guillermo is more Chango's friend
than his. No, he hasn't seen Chango either.

So when I eat a warm crunchy *bolillo*
with soft butter and strawberry preserves,
I think, *Guillermo may never taste this again.*

Or when I pass a pushcart with a hundred
pinwheels spinning rainbows,
Guillermo may never see this again.

He may never again hear the mariachi music
drifting from cafes along the *Reforma*
or smell tortillas frying in hot oil.

Every time I enjoy life,
I feel like I'm cheating on him.

                                        But then
I stand on the Padillas' flat roof and
see TV antenna coming from open windows
on the most decrepit hovels. Guillermo must have
seen how demonstrations turned violent
in Alabama, Mississippi, Chicago.

So why would he risk getting involved in a protest?
Why wasn't I more important than his causes?
My anger returns, blows up into a fiery rage.

The emotional seesaw makes my stomach ache.
Or maybe it's my heart.
A Pablo Neruda quote speaks my truth:
"Love is so short, forgetting is so long."

Luis

When he drops by,
our conversations come easily.
We sit on the curb and talk
about his Nikon camera,
the F-stops, exposures, best film,
and how to develop prints.

One day he agrees to teach me
how to enlarge a photo from a negative.
He takes me to a darkroom.
I don't mind being in the dark with him.

I consider asking him to enlarge
my photos of the shoes,
so I can look for clues
about their original owners,
but I'm afraid of putting him in danger
or of his damaging the negatives

to cover up what really happened
if his father works for the government.

So we take silly pictures, making faces
at each other, and develop them.
After I learn the process, I can do it myself,
in secret, in *The Collegian* darkroom.

Then, I can be sure my friends won't land
among the beaten, bloodied men
and women in *Lecumberri* prison.

As I hang up the wet prints
in the dim red light,
I ask him a question,
a hot topic in the US,
something I wonder about,
a culture gap between Mexican men
and me. Would my need for freedom
be understood? "What do you think
about wives working?" I ask him.

He pushes back his wire rims
and looks at me. "It's okay..."
he pauses for a beat,
"if they need to."

I ask, "What if they want to work?"

His forehead wrinkles and he tips his head
like he can't understand a woman
wanting to work outside her home.

I wonder what Guillermo would have said.
His answer might have been the same,
but there's so much I may never know about him.

White Van

Hanging out with the press staff
is always a blast.
We talk about politics in the U. S.,
fun things to do in Mexico,
the upcoming campus move to Puebla,
a provincial town outside the city.

One reporter is a proud former Marine,
who doesn't speak much, especially
about what he did in the service.

I never ask.
Maybe I don't want to know

or maybe I want to protect him
from memories that can only
be painful. Maybe both.

But he's a great listener.
After a meeting one afternoon,
our group is walking under the arches,
feet crunching across the shell-topped path,
when one of the guys asks
to see his white van, a shining star
among the clunkers in the parking lot.

He opens the back and invites us in.
The inside is as clean and spare as he is,
with his nondescript good looks.
Every brown hair in place, he always
wears a white short-sleeved shirt
and dark slacks. Brown-eyed,
unremarkable, he has a regular build
and is tall enough, but not too tall.

Five of us squeeze into the back
because his van has only driver
and shotgun passenger seats.
The only part of the van that isn't a blank
canvas is the enormous emblem
painted inside the cargo area,
a bald eagle looking to his right.
I guess it's the Marine symbol.

Maybe he bought this van
with money saved from his service.

It's cozy.
We sit in a circle and shoot the bull
as if we're around a secret campfire
where no one can see us.

I don't care that I've missed my shuttle.
Another will be by soon enough.

Five PM

When afternoon fades
into dwindling light
but night hasn't yet arrived,
an emptiness fills me.

Gone are the familiar ringing phones
from my parents' house,
the buzz of an electric can opener,
sizzle of beef in the frying pan,
blare of the evening news
from the big box TV.

Here there's nothing to distract
from creeping shadows.

In Texas my father will soon be home.
He'll stop to give my mother a quick kiss
while she, distracted, washes lettuce at the sink.

When I was there, I'd set the table,
fill glasses with milk and water,
pull out the Italian dressing,
place white bread on a melamine plate
while Libby conveniently practiced the piano
and Alan charmed Dad with his account
of an Astros game or pointed out
something funny in *Mad* magazine.

But now my sister shares
a tiny student apartment
with her husband in New Orleans,
where he is in medical school,
and I am gone too.

I don't often want to be in Texas—
my memories remind me of what was,
not what is, or what I hope will be.
But I don't know where home is any more.

I felt it once inside the cocoon of Guillermo's
arms, but now he is gone too,
and I am drifting through gray clouds
in fading skies, unsure if I can fly.

Culture Shocks

For breakfast we usually eat
eggs or refried beans with *bolillos.*
Dinner starts with *sopa de fideo,*
chicken broth with thin noodles,
and often ends with *flan,*
a sweet caramel custard, but
we never eat beef unless we're
at a restaurant. Even then, we're
more likely to get a Caesar salad
or a chicken dish. Not really a surprise
because we see lots of chickens
and goats in the country
but few cattle and not enough
green pastures to keep them fed.

So when a guy on *The Collegian* staff
asks me out to the city's A&W
for an American hamburger *and*
the root beer float I'm craving,
I'm excited about the food, the company,
and learning more about his life,
foreign to me. Darius is black
and old, in his twenties like many at UA.

Back in Texas, our synagogue made a point
of bringing diverse groups together.
It was fun meeting people from different cultures.
My parents loved that program,
but I still wasn't sure they would approve
of my going out with Darius.
They would probably talk about how hard it is
for interracial marriages to survive.

But I'm trying to move on,
and I'm not looking for serious romance
or marriage and neither is Darius.
Committed only to hamburgers, fries,
root beer floats and a good time,
we gorge on greasy food and talk
about our adventures in Mexico,
Still I definitely don't want to walk
past *Puta* Man with Darius.
God only knows what he'd shout then.

We take a different, longer route home.
As we walk and talk, he stops and says,
"I can picture you in ten years,
writing for one of those white lady's magazines."

Maybe I should be flattered, but there is something
about the way he says it that makes me wonder
if both of us have been raised with distortions.

When we get home, Luis is waiting
with the Padillas. Like Javier's other friends,
he expects for me to be there, waiting for him.
And I was not.

As I introduce "*mi amigo*" Darius
to the stone-faced Padillas and Luis,
I feel like I'm standing between high
tension wires. Luis leaves after the introduction.
Lips tight and eyes averted, instead of saying
"Hasta luego," or "Hasta la vista,"
tonight Luis says, "Adios!"

Adios

Not unexpected, he *is* American,
Darius kisses me goodnight.
But then he steps back
and makes a guttural sound
like he has scored a goal
in game I don't play.

I close the door and clomp up the stairs.
His kiss was soft, gentle,
but I didn't feel any special zing...

or want to be his hockey puck.

Two guys down in one night
            and the only key that unlocked my heart
                                    is gone.

Puzzler

In my room on the roof, I wonder
where I fit in.

More Texas peach
        than *mango de Mexico*

        prickly yellow rose
        than sunny marigold

        flower child in a flowing skirt
        than hippy with a hookah

        inquiring reporter
        than beer guzzling football fan

        eager traveler
        than fearless journalist

                Maybe I'll always be
                      alone,
                a square peg in a round
                      hole.

Phone Call

The next day there's a rare call for me.
I'm still hoping it's Guillermo,
but it's my parents.
I try to camouflage
my disappointment.

My parents will miss me, they say,
at Thanksgiving, when they will
be guests at my sister's and
brother-in-law's apartment in New Orleans.
Grandma won't travel with them
since she's recovering from surgery.

"What surgery?" I ask.

Mother says, "For the cancer, of course.
Didn't you get our letter?"

"Cancer! No, I didn't get your letter."
My voice is getting higher, louder.
"What kind of cancer?"

"Ovarian."

"Is she going to die?"

Mother hesitates. "They got most of it."
She doesn't have to say any more.
I get it. It's a bad kind.
My petite porcelain doll Grandma
probably won't live long enough
to even see me graduate.

Tears are streaming down
my face now and I'm shouting.
"Why didn't you tell me?
How can you go on and on
about a silly trip and
then casually drop this bomb?"

My father gets on the extension.
He probably could hear me screaming
from across the room.

"Don't talk to your mother that way.
This is hard enough for her.
We sent you a letter, but the damn
Mexican mail must have screwed up again."

"This isn't how we wanted
you to hear about it," Mother says.
"I'm so sorry. When you come home
in December, Grandma and all
of us will be so happy to see you."

All the grief over my grandmother
and Guillermo is like a tsunami
that sweeps me away. I can barely speak.
"Okay," I whisper. "Please tell her
I'm counting the days until I see her."
I can't say anything else.

They promise to call back in a few
days, after I, hopefully, get the letter.

We hang up, long distance calls
too expensive to pay for my silence.

Sra. Padilla pokes her pale,
worried face out the front door.
Everyone must have heard me yell
at my parents. "I'm sorry," I say.
"My grandmother is very sick
and I didn't know."

She nods and says to please let her know
if there is anything she can do to help.
Backing away, I thank her,
and run, sobbing, up the stairs.

First Letter

The letter about Grandma arrives
two days after the call,
along with her address and instructions
to send her a card. I sigh.
Always some assignment from my parents.
I don't know what to say to a dying person,
but I have plenty of questions:

While Grandma is in the hospital,
who is winding all of Grandpa's clocks,
filling Grandma's cut glass candy dish,
making her tea that's only a shade
darker than clear water?
                                           I wish
I could do all of those things for her
instead of sending empty words.

Second Letter

The University of the Americas informs me
that as a member of the newspaper staff, I have been placed on
            disciplinary warning for the rest of the quarter.

I blink and read it a second time.
It's in English, but it may as well
have been in Sanskrit. I'm having
trouble catching my breath as I see

the notice is typed on official paper.
This is not a sick prank, and I don't
have a clue why we're in so much trouble.

Has someone been watching us,
                    reporting us as a threat?
        Did Jon give me all the photos or has he revealed some to others?

Sister Cecilia? Surely a nun wouldn't tell anyone
        about Guillermo.   Would she?

                    Someone else in the Press Room?
Was the guy with the van really a Marine
        or something else?   FBI?   CIA?

What-ifs come at me from every direction:
If my parents get this letter,
        will they let me come back in January?
                    Will everyone at UA know I'm in
                    trouble?

Will I be able to transfer to a U.S. university?

        And the biggest question of all:
                    Will I "disappear" too?

Not Going to Lie...

I am sick of crying,
way past heartbreak.
Now I'm furious,
fire-breathing-dragon mad—
at cancer,
at my parents,
at school administrators,
at anyone who carries a weapon.

Natalie, Melinda, and I decide
  there's only one thing to do—drink.

We go out to a fancy cafe,
order Caesar salads with Cuba Libres.
        It doesn't help.

One of the waiters
looks so much like Guillermo
that I wonder if they're related.
I take out Guillermo's photo and ask.

"Put that away," Natalie hisses.
"What are you thinking?"

Oh, yeah. Who knows who's watching?

The waiter simply shakes his head no,
and brings us extra *bolillos* and butter.
        That doesn't help either.

"So tomorrow you march right in
and give the dean a piece of your mind."
Melinda says, slurring her words a bit.
        As tiny as she is, she can get tipsy
        after two sips.

"But be nice," Natalie warns.
"Tell them you're sure there
must be some mistake."

I stir the ice in my drink,
clink it against the glass,
wince as I bite the lime...
and my tongue.
        Nothing quenches my anger.

Eye Openers

The next morning as I dress for school,
I look in the mirror.
My hair hangs limp around my face,
and shadows circle my dull eyes.
At home I was always what others expected
me to be, but I'm not that person anymore.

I've tried so many new things,
but keep getting swatted down.
I let myself fall for Guillermo, then lost him.
I've seen children sell bloody shoes

stolen from the dead,
learned Grandma is dying too.

My hand rests on my stomach, upset
from all the drama and confrontation.
Probably the drink last night didn't help either.
Regardless, today I've got to talk to the dean,
solve my own problems,
figure out what's going on
so I don't vanish too.

Marrionettes

The dean can't see me today—he's in meetings,
but his secretary books an appointment
for me to talk with him...in three days.

My press buddies,
however, already have the scoop.
A group distributed unsigned letters
all over campus, accusing the press staff
of fiscal fraud, a charge that leaves me bewildered.

At our meetings we only talk about our articles.
Except for our faculty advisor purchasing paper,
pens, and photo development supplies,
we don't spend any money.
            But the truth doesn't matter.
            Within hours "The Administration"
            distributes a response to the student body:

"Upon the request of many Students,"
I doubt it. Most are totally indifferent,
and whoever wrote this was so ignorant
that they didn't even know not to capitalize
"students," a common noun.
"...the Administration has carefully examined
the activities of the Newspaper Staff,
with the following results:

1. No evidence of fraud has been found.

2. There is substantial evidence of unauthorized
 activity and fiscal irresponsibility."

What? There must be a hidden agenda here.
                                    But what?

The letter goes on to describe
actions taken by the administration.
The editor has been suspended
for the school session and lost his scholarship.

All of the rest of us are put on disciplinary
warning for the remainder of the quarter.
What the letter doesn't say—
the "ex-Marine" reporter with the white van
has disappeared, leaving me to wonder
who he really was.

Before he returns to the states with his wife
and family, the *Collegian* editor leaves a note for me.
"Don't let 'the man' get you down."
But it does.
I have unanswered questions
that gnaw their way to my very core.

Face-Off

On Friday, I finally meet with the dean.
He leans back in his padded chair
and smiles like a benevolent king.
In the sunlight spilling from his high windows,
dust motes cascade from books
                        shelved behind him.
I ask the dean,
"Why am I on disciplinary warning?"

He waves away my question
        "Don't worry about it," he says.

Does Dean Gottfried think I won't notice
                he's not addressing the problem?

"Have you notified my parents?"
Thinking of how disappointed they'd be
                twists

133

my stomach into knots.

He says, "You'll be in the clear
at the end of the quarter
when grades go home."

"Is this going on my record?"
That could affect my transferring
to another college or getting a job.
He shakes his head and pulls himself closer to his desk.
I half expect him to pat me on my head.
"Everything will be fine."

I stare at him. "Then why
am I on disciplinary warning?
What did I do wrong?"

He looks down and shuffles
through some papers
like he has much more
important things on his mind
than an annoying freshman girl.

I wave the letter to students outlining
our punishments, "Why
would the school investigate the newspaper
staff on the basis of an unsigned letter
and then punish some of the student editors
when
there is
no evidence
of fraud?"

"Miss Greene, we are guests in Mexico.
Being outspoken or questioning
what happens here
is not recommended."

He pushes back his chair
and walks to the door.
"As I have said, you are in the clear.
No reason to be troubled about this."

The dean opens it and makes a gesture
for me to leave, "And now I need to prepare for my next meeting."

I walk out,
       past his secretary and her pasted-on smile,
       crumple up the letter to students,
              and throw it in the trash.

People sit on the sunny lawn and talk,
       but I wonder if this campus is all
              a facade.
       We're at the mercy of whichever way
       the political winds blow.

           I hate being a chess piece in a game
           I don't know how to play.

Does the dean think I'm too stupid to understand
       he refused to answer a simple question?
And he scolded me for asking it
       like I'm a child,
       not a person whose future is at stake.

I kick some gravel down the tiered sidewalk.

I know
       unless I question and search for the truth,
I'll always be a bird with clipped wings
              trying to fly.

PART III: TRUTH OR DARE

"...violence that silences every last voice raised in protest."

Octavio Paz
Massacre in Mexico

"He thought that in the beauty of the world were hid a secret. He thought the world's heart beat at some terrible cost and that the world's pain and its beauty moved in a relationship of diverging equity and that in this headlong deficit the blood of multitudes might ultimately be exacted for the vision of a single flower."

Cormac McCarthy
All the Pretty Horses

Night Whispers

That night I can't sleep.
I sit on the cool tile floor
in the bathroom and pour
out my feelings in my journal.
I wasn't raised to be a quitter...
                        at anything.

My parents insisted I complete what I started—
swim team with a chlorine allergy
that kept me red-eyed and sneezing
for one long summer,
trigonometry class
when I wanted to drop it
                        for creative writing,
        Junior Cotillion when I didn't care
which fork was which, or how to set a table.

So I can't quit writing
                for *The Collegian.*
        Reporting is what I'm meant to do,
        but what will it cost me
and what will my parents say if I'm suspended.

Guilt whispers in one ear.
Fear in the other.
And I'm stuck in the middle.

To-Do List

I can't believe it.
        Seven hundred and fifty miles from home
        and my parents still send me
        a list of trivial chores,
        right before finals.

This time they want me
        to do holiday shopping,
        and they leave nothing to my imagination.

"When we went on our honeymoon in Acapulco,"
Dad says, "Mom got a pair of *huaraches* she loved.

She'd be so pleased if you brought her the sandals,
                    size 8 1/2 narrow."
Half sizes, narrow widths?
I wish he were kidding.

Mom is equally "generous" in her requests.
"We'd love to get guitar lessons for Alan;
          it would be such a self-esteem builder.
               Please buy a guitar there,
                    where the prices are low."

How am I supposed to get it home?

"And a ceramic pitcher for your sister.
          I noticed at Thanksgiving
          that they were short on those.
A leather wallet or bookends would be lovely
for Dad,
          and for Grandma, maybe
               an onyx vase for flowers.
By all means, buy yourself
          some of that lovely cotton lace
                    for your trousseau.
Do you have enough cash on hand?"

Shopping

For months, I've wandered through Mexican
markets, but I haven't bought much.
All those years of socking away money
so I could fly far away for college
have made me a careful shopper
or as Melinda would say, "Cheap."

Natalie says it's more that I'm afraid
to haggle, and she's right. I'm not
sure my Spanish is up to it
and don't want to pay tourist prices.

Since my roommates *want* to shop,
as opposed to my being *told* to shop,
we decide to visit the Toluca market,
hop on a bus that winds around mountains,

up and up through clouds to almost
9,000 feet, where the thin air is cooler.

The Friday market is famous
and we're armed and ready,
wallets bursting with wads of pesos
held close to our bodies.
Tented stalls fill the central street
with canvas arms stretching down alleys.

In spite of the warning that tourist
traps are located near the bus station,
Melinda buys right away.
More methodical, I pull out a small spiral
and write down prices so I can come back
and buy from the best-priced vendor.
Natalie laughs at both of us, but then
her parents didn't send her a shopping list.

At one stall, the merchant sees me recording prices,
and says, "You don't have to do that.
I'll give you the lowest price."

I laugh. "The lowest price?
I don't think so. You can tell I'm a *gringa.*"

He flashes a smile and lifts
a white cotton lace dress.
"Here. A dress that's perfect for you.
Only 100 pesos."

"Take it," whispers Natalie. "That's eight dollars."

"Bueno. Gracias." After I give him the pesos,
he hands it to me and engages Melinda and Natalie
in friendly banter. "This kind of dress is called a
Mexican wedding dress."

"A Mexican wedding dress," echoes Melinda as
someone behind her catches
my eye. I can only see his profile,
but I'd know it anywhere. "Guillermo!"

Hide-and-SSeek

He's alive!
Heart fluttering,
I slip between the girls and the stall,
joy rising as I follow his white shirt
through crowds full of them.

It must be him.
He moves with a dancer's grace,
reminds me of how I melted
in his strong arms.

Maybe he's been in hiding,
and left the city until it's safe
for him to return and contact me.
But why isn't he stopping
when I call his name?
He knows my voice.

He turns right, down a narrow alley,
shadowy under the canvas even in midday.
Stalls along this arm of the market
don't carry the usual clay pots,
silver jewelry, wool blankets.

The smells of overripe fruit and filleted fish
assault me as I call ahead, "Guillermo!"
A banana woman, smoking a pipe,
turns to stare, but Guillermo doesn't look my way.

Is he moving faster now, trying to get away?

At the end of the alley,
the market opens into a decaying
metal building where chicken heads
and animal bones hang at the entrance.

My stomach twists.
I want to pivot and run away,
back to the sunshine,
but I can't leave Guillermo.
I'm gaining on him and won't stop,

even with a stitch in my side.

As he turns a murky corner, I run
  d
    i
      a
       g
        o
          n
            a
             l
              l
            y,
                 leap over baskets
                       of *chiles,* nuts and herbs
                           to cut him off.

Gasping, I arrive
at an intersection and block
                  his
                  way.

                          Looking to his right,
                          he sidesteps me,
                          says in a smoker's
                          gravelly voice,
                          "Perdoname."

Lost

It is not Guillermo.
I have been chasing a stranger.

Only then do I hear screeches sound overhead.

up.
look
I

Birds call out harsh warnings,
flutter frantically   through broken
windows near the ceiling
as they try to find
a way out.

I turn my eyes away,
try to un-see
shards of glass shred
their scarlet-streaked wings.
Their terror feeds mine.

And now, I am lost,
trapped in a putrid smelling maze,
my Mexican "wedding" dress
clenched in one hand,
splattered with blood and feathers.

Counting My Loses

I'm not sure how long it takes
for me to find my way out
of the decaying metal building,
whether it's sweat or tears
that wet my face, but when
I find some light, I sink down
on an empty crate and cover
my eyes with my hands.

For months now
I've been looking for Guillermo,
feeling like Alice in Wonderland,
not knowing who to trust.
Now I can't even trust myself.
Maybe he didn't love me.
Maybe the day he disappeared
he was calling to break it off.

Mexico has defeated me:
I ran through armed troops
like a naive *gringa*,
and got slapped with a disciplinary warning
for reasons I can't imagine.
My Spanish is still pathetic,
and I'm chasing phantoms

like a crazy person,
a total failure at standing on my own.

My relationships with guys
have all been catastrophes.
Guillermo, Jon, Luis, Darius—
all gone. At least Luis taught me
how to enlarge photographs,
a gift mine to keep.

Wiping my eyes, I look up.
Blank-faced people walk around me,
keep their distance from the red-eyed
drippy-nosed American girl
in the hot pink mini-skirt,

All except the old man at the fish stand
who grins at me like the Cheshire Cat.

I take a deep, shaky breath and stand up.
Natalie and Melinda will be worried
and I don't know how long I've been gone
or how far I am from the bus station.
My dusty watch tells me it's after one.
We leave at two. Time to find my way back.
I've had enough of dark streets.

Gifts

We meet at the depot.
Melinda's string bags bulge
while Natalie has her purchases tucked
snuggly into a striped wool shoulder bag.
They take one look at my face and know.

I'm grateful for Melinda's relief
and Natalie's silence.
Biting my lip to steady my trembling chin,
I nod my thanks and pat my last minute stash—
two wallets, two vases, and a pitcher.
No guitar or half-sized *huaraches*
from my parent's impossible list.

On the bus, I welcome the noise from the engine,
too loud for us to talk. I need the solitude,
the rocking ride to calm myself down
and consider what I should do next.

My roommates have been my only
rock steady friends. Without any "help"
from Mother and Dad, I decide
what Christmas presents to give Natalie
and Melinda. I'll book *The Collegian* darkroom,
blow up negatives from our Chapultepec Park
picnic, and frame them for keepsakes.
All on my own.

Starting a War

Although Natalie waits for a possible visit
from Javier, Melinda comes with me
to buy printing supplies for the photographs.
She doesn't suspect a thing because I tell her
I need them for a journalism final.

Once we finish at the photo shop,
we walk next door to Sanborns,
where we can spend hours shopping
American-style for laundry soap packets,
lipsticks, postcards, socks, frames,
whatever we need...or want.
This time we hit pay dirt in the toy section—
pink and yellow plastic water pistols.

We fill them with water from the pool
at the base of a fountain on the *Reforma.*
Like little kids set free after a morning in church,
we chase through city streets, squirting each other,
a perfect way to let off steam before finals.
Squealing each time we're shot,
we turn down our street, where *Puta* Man,
face contorted with rage, runs out to scream at us.

This time I don't think. I react
in a way I never have before.
I squirt him with the gun and laugh.
Puta Man stops,
open-mouthed, his red face petrified
with what—shock, fear, anger?
as I dance backwards down the street
laughing at my power to silence him.
I'm fearless, Diana the Huntress
racing through mythical forests

until I see the usually impulsive Melinda
wide-eyed and panting. Her look stings
as I remember the truth—we're students
in Mexico, unseen dangers
                              everywhere.

Puta Man hated me before;
now I've given him a reason to attack me.
I have no idea what he might do next.

Footsteps

A few nights later, the noises start
as soon as we turn out the lights.

    The footsteps last for hours
back   forth
                and
back   forth
across the length of the rooftop deck
        outside our door.

We huddle together on Natalie's
bed, farthest from the door, and
whisper to each other in hushed voices.
If it were someone climbing
the stairs inside the house, we would
hear them open the door to the outside,
but we haven't heard anything.

We wonder if it's possible to jump
from flat roof to flat roof, if the houses
are close enough together.

Melinda thinks *Puta* Man is coming
for me. Between the roof and us,
there is only one thin wooden door,
easily splintered, and no window screens
on the sliding doors to the balcony.
Puta Man may have seen us enter this house,
but could he know we live on the roof?

Natalie says that the Padillas might
know the man, use his shoe repair,
chat with him about us, but I can't imagine
those sweet people dealing with him at all.

Since I'm the one who started this trouble,
I tiptoe to the doors and windows,
make sure they are locked.
Eventually I fall into an uneasy sleep,
dream that I am stuck in a canyon,
spend the night trying to climb my way out
over jagged rocks.

Sleepless Night 2

It happens again the next night.
Natalie pulls a broom out of the closet
and starts for the door.

"What are you thinking?" Melinda yells,
grabbing her nightgown and pulling her back.
"If the guy has a gun or knife,
what good is a broom?"

Natalie struggles to get away.

"Stop!" Melinda screams.
"You didn't hear that guy
or see his face. I did.
He's a time bomb."

I want to put my head under a pillow,
to wish this all away, but I can't
because I'm the idiot who started it.
I jump to my feet and barricade
the door. "She's right, Natalie.
It's open season on students here."

She fixes me with her usual
"You're paranoid" look.

For once, Melinda backs me up.
"I hunt," she says. "Trust me.
Between our door and the one to the stairs,
we're sitting ducks. That guy could mow you down
before anyone could get through the front gate."

Natalie's face reddens.
"Well, thank you for that image!"
She plops down on the floor.

Back against the door,
I slide down too.

Tiny Melinda stands there
hands on hips, frowning at us.
It's hard to take her seriously
when she's wearing her
Frito Bandito pajamas.

Seconds later, we're all collapsed
on the tiles, laughing and crying
from terror and exhaustion.

Melinda is the first to stop, hiccupping
as she says, "Let's sit tight tonight
and tell the Padillas in the morning.
They'll know what to do."

I imagine gentle Sr. Padilla
sitting in the dark on the drafty roof,
his cigarette tip glowing
like a night light.
There has to be another way.

I say, "I don't want to get them involved."

"No, you don't want them to know
what a dumb thing you did,"
Natalie pulls a tissue from her pocket
and blows her nose.

"Okay, Miss-Know-It-All, you're right.
Does that make you happy?"

Natalie shakes her head.
Her eyes are even more bloodshot
than the night she drank too much tequila.

We've got finals this week.
If we don't get some sleep,
all three of us will flunk out.
And I came to Mexico to be Diana
the Hunter, not Diana the Hunted.
I've got to *do* something.

Finally I say, "I have an idea."

Melinda groans.

"I'm going to put my hard shell
typewriter case on the toilet lid.
When you turn out the lights
and the noise starts again,
I'll climb up and look out
the high window."

Her olive skin pale, Natalie
leans against the wall with a blank
expression on her face.

Melinda thinks for a minute and says,
"Worth a try." She pulls out a suitcase
and sets it on top of the toilet seat.
"I'll wait in here with you
and steady you as you climb."

I'm not that big, but if I fell on
Melinda, she'd still be flattened.
Regardless, her face tells me
it isn't open for discussion.

"Sure," I say. "Natalie, turn off
the light and go back to bed.
We've got this."

"Right," she says, shooting me
a skeptical look, but she struggles
to her feet and climbs into bed.
Sitting on the cold tiles, we wait.
Not five minutes later, the thumps
start up. I giggle, something weird
I do when I'm totally terrified.

Melinda elbows me. "Shh."

"I'm sorry," I whisper. "This reminds me
of that Three Stooges routine—
'Slowly I turned. Step by step...'"

"Help me, Jesus," Melinda says.
"Are you losing it again?"

I take a deep breath. "No."
I say in a shaky voice.
"Let's do this."

She braces the heavy case while I climb
on top. I stretch up, grasp the window
sill for balance, and wait.

For my eyes to adjust to the moonlight.
For the man to walk to this side of the roof.
I hear scuffling but see nothing.

Then there's a movement down low.
I squint and focus.

Something the size of a possum
noses around the wash-tub.
How did it get up here?
Weren't the buildings too
far apart to bridge the gap?
"It's some kind of animal,
not a man!" I whisper to Melinda.

"You're kidding," she says.
"Those footsteps sound so heavy.
Are you sure it's not somebody?
Let's switch places so I can see."

But then *I* see it more clearly
and the hair on my arms
stands straight up. I jump off
the suitcase, landing on Melinda's
foot in the tight bathroom.
"Oh-my-God!" I scream.
"It's a rat! A black one
and it's a foot long."

I grab Melinda's hand and run,
her cursing me with every painful step.
Once again we land in Natalie's bed.

The Next Morning

We warn Carolina when she's serving
our breakfast not to go to the roof,
tell her how we slept all night with the lights on.
"Don't come to visit us," we say,
"until we're sure the rat is gone. It's a beast."

She doesn't need convincing, begs us
to ask the Padillas to kill it before
she has to wash clothes up there again.

We wait for Sr. Padilla, who takes one look
                at our faces (by now we probably look like
characters from the Day of the Dead parade)
and promises to have someone set traps today.

"It's the subway construction," he says,
"driving up sewer rats."

He tries to reassure us, but to me,
it's just another horror movie.
Now we'll be waiting for the snap,
squeal and scratch of dying rats.

I'm so ready to go home for the holidays,
to sleep safe in my own bed,
far from sewer rats and *Puta* Man,
marching troops and massacres,
questions without answers,
reminders of what I found...and lost.

The Letter That Arrives That Afternoon

Dear Diana,

*We are counting down the days
until you arrive. You'll love
what we've done to your bedroom.
We got rid of that old, lumpy bed
and got a brand-new sleeper sofa!
There's an armchair for reading,
a coffee table, and, of course,
the built-in desk and bookshelves.
Now it's a study by day
and a bedroom at night.
See you soon, sweetheart.
We can't wait!*

*Much love,
Mother*

I crush the letter in my fist.
I hate to admit how much I've missed them,
obviously more than they missed me
since they couldn't wait to erase
any private space I ever had at home.
Is any part of me left there?

153

Dark Room 2

The light glows red
as the pictures surface
in the chemical bath.

First Natalie and Javier
come to life, laughing
as she picks crumbs
from his moustache.

After I move the photo
from developer to fixer,
I expose and enlarge
a second one, put
the paper in the wash.
I watch Melinda
and Chango emerge.
She's pointing at the
camera, talking,
while he turns a love
struck face toward her.

It's like an assembly line—
now Natalie's photo hangs
to dry, and Melinda's
goes in the fixer. I hold
negatives in my hand,
consider what to enlarge next,
if I'm finally ready to see
what I've suspected all along.
After the market disaster,
I no longer trust my memories.

I surrender to the enlargements I fear the most,
my clearest shot of the bloody shoes,
and hope it's less threatening in black and white.
As the paper slips beneath the chemicals
I put down the tongs and rub my tired eyes.

I sigh, reopen them
and focus on the photo.
As the shoes swim to the surface
of my consciousness, one
in particular calls to me.
I blink and look again
as inked numbers emerge

along the rubber base of a canvas shoe,
but the digits are too small to read.

It's hard to breathe
as I return to the enlarger,
blow it up again,
and wait, every muscle
in my body now tight.
I move paper,
hang fixed photos.
My head spins
from the chemicals
or from fear.
I'm afraid to look.
Afraid not to.
I make myself watch them emerge,
the digits coming into focus,
ones I have been afraid to see,
the Padillas' phone number.

There Is Pain

beyond tears.
Dry-eyed, I enlarge
photo after photo
of Guillermo's shoe
until the new editor
bangs on the door

"Hey, Diana!
Are you taking a *siesta?*

"I'll be right out." My voice
sounds choked, hoarse.

"You okay?"

I want to shout, "No! I'm not.
And I'll never *ever* be okay again."

But I am in the press room
and the prints could send my friends—
students and staff—into the streets
                    to pursue a truth that could kill them.

My fists tighten, knuckles whiten
nails press into my tender palms.
I hold back a wail.
"Right out!" I gasp.

"Good," he says.
"I need to lock up.
Final tomorrow."

I rip down the prints,
bury their truth in layers
of paper towels
pack them away
in my book bag.

No one can see them.
Not here.
Not now.
Not today.

Broken Wings

Alone, I cross the crushed
shells and wait
by the dusty highway
for the school shuttle.

How empty I feel.
Deep down
I think I've always known
I would never see Guillermo again.

But hope
is like the birds
in the Toluca market,
beating their wings
against shards of glass
from shattered windows
staining rafters with blood.

As long
as they can,

the doves struggle
to find a way out,
                to fly
                    through thin
                            mountain air
                                    into the light.

On the Shuttle

I press my lips together,
lean my head back, close my eyes,
press the bag of prints to my chest.

I don't dare look at anyone,
risk my eyes revealing my grief,
or open my mouth to the cries
                    that rise inside me.

Every day we travel
the length of Chapultepec park,
watch lovers walk hand-in-hand.
Today
I can't.

I Hear

            the rattle and lurch
            of the bus rocketing
            down the pitted highway,
            whisper of the wind
            through the open windows,
            a crinkle of a candy wrappers
            from the girls across the aisle,
            punch line of a dirty joke
            told by a grunting guy,
            thump and whoosh of the door
            opening at the Lomas stop,
            growl of passing buses,
            raucous horns of taxis
            on the *Reforma*, unwanted
            signals that I must again
            open my eyes and find
            my way home
            alone.

End of the Line

Eyes down,
I get off the bus
and turn my back
to The Diana.

My feet pound the pavement
again,
           again,
                      again
in time with my beating heart.

My route home is erratic.
The sight of uniforms repels me
and there are *policia* everywhere.

I want to be an Aztec,
rake my nails across bare chests,
rip out beating hearts,
or explode in fiery agony
like the volcano Popocateptl,
burning everyone to ashes.

But I can't.

Mexico killed Guillermo,
stole his dreams
and those of his family.
I can't let it defeat me too.

I won't tell my roommates
what I know until after finals.
We need those college credits,
for the future,
a future that will never exist
for Guillermo.

Ripping through the closet,
I pull out a bag of tangled ribbons.
Melinda and Natalie find me
tying them, one after the other,
around a box, securing it
so they won't see the photos inside
of bloody shoes.

"Fancy present. Cool."
They ask who it's for.

"For you," I say.
For the gift of not knowing.

Again, Again, Again

The hammer of my heart
Breathe.

The thump of my feet
Move forward.

The secrets I keep
Hide them.

The swish of turning pages,
Study.

The passing out of blue test booklets
Begin.

The scratch of pencils against paper
Remember.

But not everything.
Hold back the inevitable
knowing of the finite
and the infinite.

See my reflection
in Guillermo's eyes,
laugh with him,
feel his lips on mine?
Never again.

Ghost Kisses

He visits at night while I sleep.
His breath warms my skin.
His lips brush mine, soft, light,
like the feathers that fill my pillows.
I snuggle deeper into his embrace,

but then he's gone again,
and I wake up shivering
under the click, click, click
of the ceiling fan,
my face wet with cold tears.

I
wonder
how
I will ever find
someone
to love me like that
again.

After Our Last Finals

Before I pack for the trip home,
I pull out Christmas gifts
for Natalie and Melinda,
framed and wrapped photos
of Sunday-in-Chapultepec-Park.
I had them hidden in the big box
of shoe photos, tied up tight
with many crimson ribbons to unknot,
as many as the decisions I'll have to make
about what to do with them.

Melinda, bursts through the door,
blonde curls bouncing, delighted
to have finished the quarter.
She celebrates by opening her present
right then. Natalie, always less impulsive,
saves hers for Christmas.

As she picks it up to put into her suitcase,
something falls away onto the bedspread.

"What is this?" she asks, picking up
an enlarged photo of the stained shoes.

I am suddenly cold. It must have stuck
to the bottom of her wrapping paper.

She turns her wide green eyes to me.

Before I can stop them,
words spill from my mouth,
my voice raspy from unshed tears.
"I took these near the visa office
on the day after Tlatelolco.
That's blood."

Melinda puts her hand over her mouth.
Natalie crosses herself.
I take a shuddering breath.
"There was something I missed
until last week," I say.
I point to the enlargement.
"The Padilla's phone number
on this one, Guillermo's shoe."

Now They Know Too

My voice cracks as I finally say it.
"Carolina told me the beggars sold
the shoes of the dead."

Unlike Natalie, Melinda can't look away.
She points. "Those look like Chango's
Converse sneakers, the ones with the hole
where his big toe had poked through,
but Javier said he had seen him."

Natalie whispers, "There could be lots of people
with the same shoes."

But it makes sense that Chango and Guillermo,
good friends, would be near each other at the rally.

I wrap my arms around my churning stomach
and ask Natalie, "Would Javier know Guillermo
and Chango are dead and lie to protect us?"

Anger, confusion, fear flash across her face.
"I don't know," she finally answers, raking
back her long brown hair with her hands.
"Should I show him the photo?"

"No." I'm trembling now.
"His father works for the government.
The truth is in the photo.
It might land Javier or his family in jail.
Or worse. If his father reports we have it,
we might be in danger or endanger the Padillas."

 Natalie turns to Melinda.
"When Javier and I are alone,
I'll ask him to take me to visit Chango."

"That would work," I say.
"You can watch how he reacts.
If Chango *is* safe, you can see him."

Melinda jumps to her feet and rips
her Olympic posters from the wall.
"Don't bother. I'm getting the hell out
of here and don't want to know."

Unexpected

"We're all getting the hell out of here.
Tomorrow morning," Natalie says.
"Have you forgotten we're sharing
a taxi to the airport?"

Melinda walks while she talks,
"I'm not coming back," she says
in an un-Melinda-like voice,
quiet and determined. "Ever."

She pulls her photos and teddy bear
from the shelves of the room divider
and stuffs them into a second bag.

Speechless, Natalie and I look at each other.

"I finished the quarter," Melinda says,
"so my parents can't complain about my wasting
their money, but I don't belong in this crazy country
where people kill each other for no good reason."

"Killings happen in the U.S. too," I say.

"I don't care." She goes on in a steely voice.
"In every letter, Lonnie asks me
to marry him, and I'm going to say yes."

"Lonnie?" Natalie asks.

"Her boyfriend back in Louisiana," I say.

Natalie's mouth forms an O.

I rest my head in my hands.
No, no, no! I want to shout. *Don't do it.*
Marriage is a trap. But then I think of Guillermo,
how safe I felt with his arms around me,
his cinnamon lips on mine,
what life might have been with him.

Melinda rips into the closet.
"He's got a good job as a mechanic
and I'm nineteen. I can get married whenever I want,
whether my parents like it or not."
Natalie raises her eyebrows;
There are questions all over her face.

I shake my head. How can Melinda fall
for that lie, that marriage will keep her safe?
It sure didn't work for Guillermo's mother.
Or the Kennedy women. Or Mrs. King.

My throat is so tight now that it's hard to speak.
"I'm sorry you saw that. Please come back."

She stops, swivels her head,
and makes eye contact with me.
"I'm sorry too. I just can't do this anymore."

163

Goodbyes

When Natalie and I wake the next morning
Melinda is gone. She slipped out
while we slept.

On her bed, she left the framed
picture of her with Chango
and a letter to Natalie and me.

> Dear Natalie and Diana,
>
> Sorry to sneak out, but I'm not good
> at goodbyes. It's easier this way. Please
> forgive me for leaving behind the photo,
> but since I'll soon be a married woman,
> I don't think it would be cool to keep
> a picture of me with another guy.
> Stay safe and have a good Christmas.
>
> Your homesick friend,
> Melinda

I pass the note to Natalie.
When she finishes reading it,
I say, "We're never going to hear
from her again, are we?"

Natalie shakes her head no.

"She's just going to wipe her mind
clean of everything that's happened
during the last four months
and erase us with them."
I wonder how could she
turn her back on the truth,
simply let it go,
walk away?

I rip her photo from the frame
and tear it into tiny pieces,
leaving only the image of Chango,
angry tears fill my eyes.
It takes every bit of energy
I have left to hold back sobs.

"I bet she didn't tell the Padillas
either, left it up to us," Natalie says.

I nod. "Let's talk to them after breakfast.
They may want to find a third student
while we're on vacation."

Natalie sighs, "I can tell.
it's going to be a long day."

She has no idea how long.

Breakfast

Unseen hands twist my heart
when I sit down at the telephone desk
in the hall outside the Padilla's flat.
This is where Guillermo sat
to scribble my phone number
on the rubber rim of his shoes.

I pull out the phone book
and blink away tears so I can look up
and write down an address
on a stuffed envelope which I tuck
into my woven leather purse.
I hear Natalie's footsteps
on the stairs above me.

When Sra. Padilla walks into the dining room
to wish us *Feliz Navidad* and safe travels,
Natalie is tearing her *bolillo* into tiny pieces.
I'm staring at the strawberry preserves,
my favorite, but don't have the energy
to lift my knife and spread it on the bread.
We're both eying Melinda's empty chair,
dreading telling *Señora* the news.

But she's perfectly calm.
She doesn't even seem surprised,
like her boarders run off all the time
to get married rather than return to school.
Yes, she says she will try to find us a new roommate.

We hug her and Carolina who helps us
drag our bags outside to wait for the taxi.
I keep my arms pulled tight to my body
to protect the purse that holds two packets
of photos and my airline ticket.

The negatives, wrapped in protective paper,
hide beneath the satin lining of my makeup case.
I can't risk traveling with the enlarged photos.

Waiting for the Cab

As we wait, a red-eyed Natalie asks,
"Will *you* come back?'

I take a deep breath, hesitating too long
because her eyes fill with tears.

The only thing I know for sure is that
I can't run away from everything,
like Melinda, and live with myself.

Last night, while Natalie and Melinda slept,
I took the photos into the tiny bathroom,
and sat on the tile floor,
goose bumps rising on my bare legs,
as I labeled location and date on the back
of every wrenching snapshot.

As the taxi pulls up, I turn to Natalie
and squeeze out the words.
"I'm not sure if I'll come back.
It depends on what happens today."

"What do you mean?"

"We can't talk about it now."
I cut my eyes over to the driver,
a reminder we're not alone.
He loads our suitcases into the trunk
and piles the ones that won't fit
onto the passenger side of the front seat.
My mind is made up, but I'm trembling,
sit on my hands to steady them
once we're inside.

"I have twelve hours before my flight,"
I whisper to Natalie, "and there are things
I need to do before I leave.
I'm going to have him drop me at the Hilton
on the *Reforma* so I'll pay for our ride to that point."

"Why are you stopping there?"

"I'll call you tomorrow, after we're both home,
 and tell you everything then."

I'm rocking now, trying to push through my fears,
remembering pressroom nightmare stories,
of students locked away in *Lecumberri* prison,
but I can't fall to pieces now. I can't.

 Natalie has a bruised look about her,
dark half-moons under swollen eyelids,
and I'm sure I look even worse.
"You're scaring me," she says.
 "Please promise you won't do anything stupid."

In the stuffy backseat of the cab,
I fold one leg up under me
and face Natalie, my hands clasped
tightly now over my white knee.
"I need your help."
Her face tenses.

"After Christmas, when you return to Mexico,
ask Javier if you both can meet Chango
for drinks to celebrate the New Year.
Since Melinda isn't coming back,
Javier can no longer use the excuse
that Chango is avoiding her."

"Why don't you ask him?"

I don't answer her question.
"You can see how Javier reacts.
If he takes you to see him,
you can let me know he's okay.
If Javier doesn't, see if you can find out
Chango's real name so you can give it
to your priest at confession."

Her face relaxes and she laughs.
"Oh, I thought you were serious.
You and Melinda give me such a hard time
about being a nice Catholic girl."

I'm not laughing. "No, really.
I've thought hard about this."
I glance at the driver, but he's busy
watching the traffic...and the meter.
I hope he doesn't speak English.

Wiping my shaky hands on my dress,
I say, "I don't want to put anyone in danger,
but I keep thinking about their parents,
Guillermo's and Chango's, not knowing.
Give the priest the photo of Chango
that Melinda left behind. Maybe he can find
his family. Doesn't a priest have to protect
your confidentiality?"

Natalie pulls her head back. "Yes."

"He could contact other parish priests
who might be able to find his parents."

Natalie hesitates. "You do realize millions
live in Mexico City," she says, tucking
strands of her shiny hair behind her ears.

My head throbs with unshed tears.
"If I were their mothers or grandmothers,
I would be lighting candles and praying
every day so maybe a priest can find them.
They shouldn't have to spend their lives looking
for their sons in every stranger's face. It will
make them crazy, like me in the market."

She sighs. "I guess it's worth a try,
but what about Guillermo?"

"I'll take care of that," I say.

"Oh, *please*," she says, "Don't try
to contact his family. It's too risky."

I don't say anything.

She crosses her arms and looks out
the cab window at the choked city streets.
"What's the point? Nothing you can do
will bring him back."

Her words feel like a slap.
I pick at a loose thread on my skirt,
twisting it tighter and tighter around my finger,
barely keeping it together. "I know," I say,
"but I can't do *nothing*."

I Am Still Diana

I ask the taxi driver to circle the statue
of Diana on the way to the hotel.
From Natalie's rigid posture I know
she senses I'm saying good-bye.

This was where we started our adventures.
The school shuttle picked us up here
every day at the gates of *Chapultepec* Park,
across from Diana's statue, where
bow and arrow in hand, she danced
atop the fountain's flowing waters.

I take one last look at the goddess,
desperate to capture her fluid grace,
bronze strength, and free spirit,
to find it still alive in me.

Today
will I become the hunter
or the hunted?

After only four months in Mexico,
my innocence is lost,
but, like Diana, I'm still a virgin
with my single unbroken arrow
pointed north.

Bellman at the Hilton

My arrival at the hotel happens so fast.
The bellman unloads everything—
the useless electric typewriter,
and my matching set of baby blue
luggage—make-up case, small
and large suitcases—onto the trolley.
I barely have time to pay for the taxi
and blow a kiss to Natalie who is looking
out her window and misses my goodbye.

I follow him inside the lobby,
grab a city map from the display,
and ask him to stop. "Please."
With my back to the desk, I flash
a wad of *pesos*, and ask him to store
everything until check-in time this afternoon.

"Of course, *señorita*."
He's about my age and good-looking.
With his ready smile and thick dark hair,
I'm sure he's used to big tips, but
I worry about whether I can trust him.

My hand brushes his warm palm
as I hand off his tip and walk back
to the revolving glass doors, going around
twice so I can see if he's doing what I asked.
He winks at me as he heads down a side hall.

Associated Press

Out on the sidewalk,
I'm sweating and shivering
even though it's another beautiful morning.

I take deep breaths to still my nausea
and try to focus only on what I have to do.

And then I'm walking, walking down
the tree-lined *Paseo de la Reforma*
to number eighteen, the address I found
in the Padilla's phone book for the AP.

In the days following Tlatelolco
readers turned to them, the best news
gathering source in the world,
but even their journalists found fixed
bayonets pointed in their direction,
their film destroyed.

That packet in my purse, photos
labeled by location and date
tell a story they can share
across the globe, but their offices
are barred with metal gates,
and I am only a pacing girl,
walking up and down the block,
hoping to hand off my bulging envelope
to someone entering the office
before I'm spotted by *policia*.

The Policeman on the Corner

He's copper-skinned, wears a cap
pulled low over his eyes.
Every few seconds he shakes
his oversized gold wristwatch,
one not even my father could afford.
I watch him until he begins to watch me.
I am the only young woman out alone
                          on this block.

Workmen cluck at my passing.
With each lap, my skin tightens
until I'm sure I'll burst
if someone doesn't enter #18 soon.

As I near the policemen his jangling
watch sets my teeth on edge.
I have to do something.

Then it comes to me,
soft and sure as a kiss
from Guillermo.

The next time I pass the police
I shake my head and say,
"My boyfriend is *always* late!"
His face giving away nothing,

he nods, but he doesn't track
me as closely after that.

I lean against a wall
two doors down from the AP,
check my Timex,
and flip my thick hair up
to cool my neck.

I can't forget Carolina's stories
of political prisoners at *Lecumberri* prison,
the Black Palace, where guards beat naked prisoners,
        men *and* women, rape many,
and leave them in filth for weeks.
If I fail today, I could disappear there too.

I'm wiping sweat or tears
from beneath my eyes,
when a man approaches the gate
and buzzes for it to open.

I rush toward him, shrieking,
tug on his leather shoulder bag.
It slides down his arm to the ground.
"What the hell!" he says.

"Is that any way to talk to your *novia?"*
I scream, moving closer,
unable to stop my tears.

As he bends to retrieve his bag,
I choke out the words in a whisper
"Tlatelolco photos."

His eyes open wide as I shove
                the envelope into his bag.

Then, even though the guy is way older,
                twice my age and size,
I stand up straight, slap him hard,
                and scream, *"Nunca!*
I never want to see you again."
                Then I turn and run.

Hiding in Plain Sight

I jump on the first bus
heading deeper into the city
and wedge myself upright
among a group of teenage girls.

Sides heaving, I scan faces to see
if anyone has followed me.

One man pressed against a pole
near the door looks vaguely familiar,
but it isn't the policeman
or the man from the AP.
His face gives away nothing
and I wonder if he's one of the soldiers
I ran past on that day long ago
in Chapultepec Park.

The smiling guy standing next to him
has bushy eyebrows like my dad.
I've never been able to stand up to my father,
who I'll face tonight with the unexpected
news that I won't return to Mexico in January.

He may say I'm a quitter
or believe I'm afraid to be on my own.
                                    I'm neither.

It's time to tell my parents
the truth about what I want,
about what happened in Mexico,
and how I was involved.

My parents may want to keep me
closer to home—I couldn't blame them—
but I have left before,
and I will do it again.

All my muscles ache in the packed space.
I shift my weight from one stiff leg to the other.
The bus stinks of sweat,
probably most of it mine,
but I ignore the stench
and suck in as much air as I can.

Tonight, when I'm in flight,
I'll worry about my family,
For now, I have to keep moving.

Passing *Tlatelolco:*
Plaza de las Tres Culturas

Even the name causes me pain,
but I lift my head, take a mental snapshot
of a place I've avoided for months.

Guillermo's last phone call, broken,
came from here. I'd give anything to know what
he was saying when gunfire interrupted.
What wish did he have, never fulfilled?
This is where they killed him.
God, I hope he didn't suffer.

The Aztec ruins and ancient Catholic
cathedral are still here, as they have been
for hundreds of years. The victims are not.
Not a single report, either, of priests or nuns
opening the convent gates to those fleeing
the rooftop snipers. My anger is a white hot rock
buried deep in my gut.

As workers trail out of the emptying bus
and descend the bus steps in a cloud of exhaust,
I sink onto an open seat, its maroon leather in shreds.

Again, I remind myself to breathe,
to listen for that all important stop,
the *Instituto Politécnico Nacional.*
I check my watch again.
Only a few hours left to make my flight.

Instituto Polytechnico Nacional

The *granaderos* at the gates
are checking IDs. Not good.
Not good at all.

Trying to swallow my panic
I pat the pocket in the folds
of my dress and push away the stories
from international journalists
about the continuing war
between students and government.

Lines merge, and I long to run.
Only a sprinkling of women are there,
most in white blouses and colored skirts.
I'm wearing the most conservative clothes I own,
the tailored navy blue I wore to Grandpa's funeral,
my death clothes. It's fitting, I guess,
but today I hope to honor Guillermo's life.

I move with the line, fumble through my purse,
not knowing whether it's best to show
my UA student ID or my passport.
My final decision doesn't come
until I'm facing an impassive *granadero*,
who is no taller or older than I am,
but carries a rifle with a fixed bayonet
like those I saw on the *Reforma*.

In spite of the warming day,
I shiver as I hand him my passport.
Resting one hand protectively
on my pocket, I watch him
scan the document.

"Why are you here?" the *granadero* asks.

I respond in my choppiest Spanish,
say my mother's cousin works here,
and she has asked me to give him
a photo of my sister's wedding
before I fly home to the United States.

I pull out an ivory-colored envelope,
the one that I always carry in my purse,
a wedding photo of my sister and her husband
surrounded by our family.

The guard nods, seemingly satisfied,
but flips through the pages of my passport

as the line behind me swells.

175

Oh, no, no, no.
I can see by his eyes that he notes
my student status. His eyes return to my face
and he studies me before passing off
the passport to an older, stouter man.

"American student.
Go over there," he says, pointing for me
to follow the older *granadero* so others can pass.

The air around me hums.
Black spots dance before my eyes
like they did when I fainted
in the high school cafeteria.

I shake my head hard and follow
the *granadero*. Perhaps I look as pale
as I feel or maybe he doesn't want to have
to deal with a queasy *gringa,*
because he leads me to the spotty
shade of a stringy tree.

"Why are you here?" He asks
the same question as the first.

I fan myself with the photo envelope
and repeat my story, struggling with the
Spanish. This time I add that today
I will return home from my visit.
I pull out my flight itinerary,
which seems to satisfy him,
and he gestures for me to move on.

Relief floods me
and my legs tremble as I walk
into the cool, dark recesses
of the administration building.

Inside

First I find the bathroom,
splash cold water on my face
so I can think more clearly
about what to do next.

It's not like I can go up to anyone
to ask where to find the father
of Guillermo Cordero del Rey.
A well-dressed American girl
asking where to find a maintenance
worker won't fly. I'll have to
walk the halls and hunt for him
or ask other students for help.

I don't dare ask a guy; he might
think I'm flirting and follow me
like strangers do on the streets.
A female. It has to be a female,
and there are so few here.

I dry my face
and tiptoe into the hall,
grateful that I've worn flats
rather than heels that might
click-clack across floors.

As I climb the stairs to the second floor,
a wall-eyed man with coarse dark hair
passes me and turns on the landing.
He's watching me so I drop my eyes,
pray he'll go away.

The next time I spot him,
he's outside a classroom,
I step into the shadows at a doorway
and wait in a corner until the hall goes silent.
Then I peek around the corner.
No one in sight. I can breathe again.

It takes forty-eight long minutes of walking,
hiding out in empty classrooms,
lingering in bathrooms on every floor.

Finally, an older woman
wearing a uniform with an apron

enters a bathroom and I follow her inside.
"Please tell me where can I find Mr. Rey."

"I don't know, *senorita,*" she says
and pulls a bucket and mop out of the closet.
The air is close in the bathroom,
and the ammonia fumes sting my eyes and throat.

" Do you know him?"

"Yes, but I haven't seen him."
Her hands tremble.
She's lying.
And I've got a plane to catch.
No time to waste.

I step forward, corner her.
"Tell me right now where he is!
I know his son and must talk to him.
Now!"

Her hand tightens on the mop handle.
My intensity frightens both of us.
I wonder if she'll strike me with her broom.
Tears fill my eyes.

Her eyes flicker with uncertainty
but she speaks, her voice a whisper.
No dijeran a nadie que hablamos.
Don't tell anyone we talked.
His father is fixing the water fountain
upstairs by the men's bathroom.

"Upstairs at the water fountain by the boy's
bathroom," I whisper back and put my hand
over my heart. *"Gracias, Señora. Vaya
con Dios."* I bolt for the door. When
I swing it open, there's a girl on the other side,
the only one beside the maid that I've seen
on this floor. How much has she heard?

Señor Rey

I leap up the stairs and find his father,
back bent as he stoops to tighten a u-shaped pipe.
I slow, then freeze when I see his face,

so much like Guillermo's—
thick hair framing almond-shaped eyes,
heavy brows, full lips, a mustache
that Guillermo was too young to grow,
but he moves like an old man,
hunched and slow as if he's in pain.
                    Is the information I carry
                    like the broken windows in the market,
                    bloody shards that will destroy him
                    or will it bring his family peace?
Trembling and fighting tears, I step forward,
pull out an envelope with the family photo,
say, "Good morning, Cousin!"
Voice lowered, I add, "If anyone asks,
you're my mother's cousin
looking at my sister's wedding photo."

Beneath his hooded eyes, I see no change
of expression. "I have news of Guillermo,"
I whisper. The only sign of acknowledgement
is an eye twitch as he puts down his wrench
and opens his worn fist to receive the envelope.
I look down the hall. Thank God it's empty.

I speak quickly, pull a second envelope
from my pocket and slip it under the first.
"The location and date of this photo are on the back.
The phone number on his shoe was mine.
I'm returning to the United States today,
but I want you to know he talked of you
and your family with great love and respect.
He was an honorable man." My voice cracks
as I continue, "I will never forget him."

His father shows nothing, keeps his eyes down,
but in that moment I feel great relief
that I can give Guillermo's family
the gift of knowing.

I exhale,
but then I see him,
the wall-eyed man standing in a doorway.

First Flight

Guillermo's father covers
the second envelope with the first
and pulls out the family photo.
"My cousin was a beautiful bride."

I nod, my throat too tight to speak,
and try to smile. It takes every bit
of self-control not to run.
I can't tell what the stranger sees,
which eye follows me,
until he raises his eyebrows and turns his head
toward Sr. Cordero and the wedding picture.
If he asks to see them, he'll see
my family has brown hair, but fair skin,
and Guillermo's father is clearly *mestizo*.

And Sr. Cordero needs time to hide the other
envelope, the one with the photos of bloody shoes
that could either be a bullet to destroy his family
or the salve to heal their wounds.

I release my hand so my Mexican leather bag
falls, everything inside spilling out on the floor—
passport, wallet, gold compact, Pink Passion
lipstick, luggage claim check from the Hilton.
It works.

His back to Sr. Cordero, the thin man helps me
gather my things. He boldly reads my open passport,
as Sr. Cordero slips the second envelope

into his tool box. Then he joins us,
helps me gather my scattered pesos.

I silently pray the stranger is a safe man,
that my imagination is in overdrive,
that he's not undercover and on the hunt.

"Gracias," I say to them both as I retrieve my purse.
"And now I have a plane to catch."

"Thank you for the photo," Sr. Cordero says,
and the wall-eyed man asks, "May I see it?"

I feel my false smile tighten,

I can't remember if I wrote any personal
information on the back.

Guillermo's father hands it over with a flourish,
as if everything is fine. "My cousins.
Very handsome. Right?"

The skinny guy flips it over on the back.
and studies it intently." *Sus nombres?"*
Their names?

I hold my breath until I see
nothing is written on the back.
If Sr. Cordero says names that are different
from what he read on my passport,
we're caught.

My fists tighten. "We're the Greene family
and now live in Texas. I'm Diana,
named for the huntress."

"Who is this one?" he asks Sr. Cordero
who raises his hand when I start to answer.

Sr. Cordero taps the photo with his finger.
"Why, Anna, of course."

"*Disculpame*. I'm sorry." My voice cracks.
"If I don't leave right now, I'll be late for my flight.

"It was good to see you, Cousin.
Please give my best to my cousins. "

Eyes swimming with tears that threaten to spill,
I turn my back to them and pray with each step
that Sr. Cordero and his family will be safe.

Once, when I am crossing the landing
to a flight of stairs, I think
I see the stranger descending
from above, but then he disappears
as I run out the door.

"Don't Run!"

yells the older *granadero*
who lifts his rifle as I rush
out of the building.

I stop, raise my hands, knowing
students have been killed for less.
Long seconds pass before I can breathe.

With a lowered head, like a dog that fears a beating,
I finally whisper, "I'm sorry. I forgot."

Bordering the walkway, dahlias bob their heads
and pigeons peck at the ground near my feet,
but I'm rooted in place.

The *granadero* frowns,
but lowers his weapon.
"Don't you forget."

As if I ever could.
Somehow I get my feet moving
again and walk stiffly to the curb.

Not a taxi in sight, I take the first bus
that arrives, not caring where it goes.
As we pull away, I look back, and see
the wall-eyed man pointing at me
and talking to the *granadero*.

Reforma

When the bus crosses
the *Reforma*, I get off.
        Lightheaded, I still don't feel safe,
        can't even remember the last time
        I felt safe. I'm always looking
        over my shoulder. My first stop
        is the bank. More armed guards.
Heart pounding, hands sweating,
I withdraw all my hard-earned savings
except for five dollars and list *Puta* Man's
shoe repair as my forwarding address
for any bills that haven't yet cleared,
my revenge for all the times
he called me a whore.
        Today the money meant for an adventure
        will pay for a disguise. I weave in
        and out of packed stores, buying
        sunglasses, a straw hat and an aqua
        cotton dress embroidered in bold colors,
        the kind of clothes tourists wear.
Then I walk into the lobby of a random
hotel and change my clothes in a restroom.
I tuck my hair up into the hat,
and put on the sunglasses before
I check myself out in the mirror.
        I'm dressed like a true *gringa,*
        a person that I vowed I'd never be
        when I arrived in Mexico.
My eyes fill with tears;
knowing that beneath the disguise,
I've changed.
        Feeling lighter than I have
        in a long,
                  long
                        time,
I walk to the Hilton,
but my heart hurts for the Corderos,
who now know
they have lost their only son.

        I want to go home.

The Hilton

I hesitate at the revolving doors.
The wall-eyed man saw my claim ticket
when I dropped my purse and might track me here.
Stepping to one side, I pull
            it from my purse.
Relief floods me when I see the hotel name
is nowhere on the ticket, just a number.

The first bellman is nowhere around.
I ask another one for my luggage,
give him a different story
about an early check-out, late flight,
and tip him well in spite of the fact
a bra strap hangs from my largest suitcase.
Someone has been through my things.

I don't know if anyone saw the negatives
under the lining in my make-up case,
but I doubt they have been stolen.
The photos might set off alarms,
endanger me among *granaderos,*
but they would mean nothing to someone
more interested in jewelry or cash.
They would find neither in my things,
but this is still a final violation,
a stranger's hands on my underwear.

I tell myself that it's okay—
that today I did what had to be done,
that Sr. Cordero now knows what happened
to his son, that love and respect remain.

In the Taxi

                        up
Realization floats

                and I am,
                        afraid again.

I showed my itinerary to the *granadero.*
        Now he knows
                I am going.
                        to the airport.

184

As the taxi pulls up to Departures,
I tuck my hair tight into my hat
        and pull it as low as I can.

                Porters scurry around, claiming
                suitcase-carrying privileges,
                but I keep my head down,
                tip any outstretched hand.
                There's no avoiding
                standing in line
                to check
                bags.

                        Wound as tight as Grandpa's chiming clocks,
                        I flinch at any movement around me,
                        receive my ticket and claim checks
                        with trembling hands.

Oversized sunglasses in place,
I try to casually walk to my gate
with my make-up case in one hand,
electric typewriter in the other
(Why-oh-why didn't I check it?)
and purse strap slung over one shoulder.

The damn typewriter slams against my thigh
                with every step
as I pass armed guards
        near the *Aeronaves de México* gates,
                but there are none visible
                at the Pan Am gate.

Not taking a chance
I hide out in the bathroom
crack open the door to listen
for boarding announcements
emerge only when the departure gate
opens and the line dies
                down.

This is it.
My final dash
toward family
and safety.

                        As I climb the steps
                        to board the plane, I look back,
                        unsure if my fears distort my vision
                        or if the wall-eyed man stands
                        in the airport shadows.

185

When the Pan-Am Hatch Closes

That final metallic thump
sounds like the dropping of a lid
on a concrete burial liner.

Something in me breaks open,
and I sob with relief and sorrow
and so much more.

As the stewardess walks down the aisle
checking seat belts, she pats my shoulder
with her white-gloved hand

and passes me a package of tissues.
She must have seen more than a few
heartbroken people leave Mexico.

Sealed in this in-between place
I can't hide from the enormity
of what I'm leaving behind.

The plane picks up speed on the runway,
and I look through the round windows
as final images of Mexico flash by.

Then we lift off and hurtle into the clouds
away from the bold music, spices,
and colors of the city Guillermo and I loved.

On the Other Side

At home, I want to crawl into my childhood bed
                              and sleep for days
But my bed is gone.
And so is my childhood.

It's time.
I have to find the courage to tell me parents.
                              the truth.
About what I want.
About Guillermo.
About what I now know.

I'm losing my independence
until fall when maybe I can transfer to a university
if I squeeze in enough courses at a local college.

At first, I'll need my parents' approval again
for anything I want to do; my dwindling savings
won't cover much in the U.S., but I can work.

They might not want me to leave again,
to travel abroad junior year and beyond,
but I've done it before and I can do it again.

And in the States, I can speak up, share the photos,
write what I saw, the bloody pyramid of shoes,
each a reminder of an injured or lost life.

Reverse Migration

As the plane ascends sharply to clear mountains,
we hit air pockets with deep drops
and steep rises.

Moans and exclamations surround
me as the plane dips to one side
like a bird with a broken wing.
My electric typewriter slides
in and out from under the seat,
slamming into my toes.

This time I'm the one praying,
praying to see my family again.
I want to hug and be hugged, laugh and argue,
crack warm pecans with Dad's silver nutcracker,
drink Cokes and munch on Mom's Chex mix,
ask Libby about teaching and her marriage,
convince Alan to let me read his MAD magazines,
tell my grandmother I'll always love her.

Lights blink off and on
while the plane creaks and groans.
Thrown this way and that,
I want to go home.

Like Mexico, my family cares about appearances,
        but never at the cost of those unseen things
            rarely discussed,
                what truly matters.

                                        And if I'm wrong,
                                        I can change that.
                                        It can start with me.

Nightfall

Exhausted, I fall asleep
moments after the plane
levels off.

I dream I kiss Guillermo's warm lips
at the gates of Chapultepec Park.
We untangle hands, touch fingertips
one last time.

Then I'm floating north over the desert,
wrapping crystalline memories,
layer after layer, in tissue,
like a wedding dress never worn.

My arms form an X
across my chest as bands of loss
grow tauter with each mile.
Thorny cactus, limbs outstretched,
reach up towards early stars
veiled in last light.

So many wings come here dipping honey and speak here in your home
                    Oh God.
                — Aztec Poem

Corrido de Dolor

Escuchen la triste historia.
Hoy nuestros corazones se quiebra.
Escuchen la triste historia.
Sus corazones también se quiebra.

Es el dos de octubre del ano
mil novecientos sesenta y ocho.
En la Plaza de las Tres Culturas,
bengalas iluminan la noche.

Los helicópteros dan vueltas.
Las garras del águila rasgan el cielo.
Rayos caen sobre la tierra
Pistolas truenan. Las nubes lloran.

Francotiradores en posición.
en la Guardia Presidencial
disparan desde los techos.
La serpiente se come a sus crías.

Matan a gente—joven, vieja—
que sólo quieren hablar y vivir.
Nunca hay suficientes lágrimas.
para lavar la sangre carmesí.

Por la Pirámide Tlatelolco
como temidos dioses Aztecas
exigiendo sacrificios,
Matan a cientos de personas

Un río de sangre joven fluye
por las puertas barricadas, fuertes,
de la iglesia católica
de Santiago de Tlatelolco.

Esconden a los muertos, heridos,
Encarcelan más de mil testigos.
No decimos nada. ¡Tanto miedo!
¿Nos matarán a nosotros despues?

Durante los Juegos Olímpicos,
vestimos nuestras mejores ropas
y sonreímos para el mundo
                    Escondemos nuestro dolor.

Song of Sorrow

Listen to the sad story.
Today our hearts are broken.
Listen to the sad story.
Your hearts will break too.

It's October 2, the year
nineteen sixty-eight.
In the Square of Three Cultures,
flares light night.

The helicopters spin around.
Eagle talons rip sky.
Lightning strikes earth.
Guns thunder. Clouds cry.

Restless snipers
from the Presidential Guards
shoot from rooftops.
The snake eats its young.

They kill people—young, old—
who only want to speak their truth.
There are never enough tears.
to wash away the crimson blood.

By the Tlatelolco Pyramid,
like feared Aztec gods
demanding sacrifices,
they kill hundreds of people.

A river of young blood flows
by the strong barricaded doors
of the Catholic church
Santiago de Tlatelolco.

Mexico hides the dead, the injured,
imprisons more than a thousand witnesses.
We say nothing. So much fear!
Will they kill us later?

During the Olympic Games,
we put on our best clothes
and smile for the world
                    We hide our sorrow.

Afterword

Some stories take fifty years to surface. *On Wings of Silence* is one of them.

The first readers to recognize the significance of this topic were Anne McCrady and 2008 Texas Poet Laureate Larry D. Thomas, who selected my poem "Chapultepec Park" for the 2008 Christina Sergeyevna Award at the Austin International Poetry Festival. When critique partner Joy Preble said she believed there was a novel hidden within that poem, I began to search for answers to lingering questions about the chaos prior to the 1968 Olympics. Dr. Cliff Hudder, my earliest b
Beta reader, directed me to Elena Poniatowska's *Massacre in Mexico*, and Alicia Salazar, whose uncle survived the bloodbath, contributed as a sensitivity reader.

Other Beta readers of the full manuscript included Dr. Molly McBride, Dianne Logan, Juan Paloma, and Kim O'Brien. Their insights, as well as critiques by Bob Lamb and Suzanne Bazemore, along with inspirations from Charles Trevino's SCBWI "Critique Critters" at Lone Star College improved my storytelling. Fellow author Kathryn Lane helped with the wording of the Spanish version of the *Corrido*. I am especially grateful to my mentor and friend Dave Parsons, 2011 Texas Poet Laureate, who helped me develop my poetic voice.

For a quarter century, the *Tlatelolco* tragedy remained buried. With increasing access to Internet data, I eventually confirmed my worst fears; Communist instigators encouraged the student protests and the United States sent weapons and ammunition to Mexico to quell any conflict.

When former Mexican President Luis Echeverria spoke up about the young victims of the massacre, he said, "These kids were not provocateurs. The majority were the sons and daughter of workers, farmers and unemployed people." According to him, then President Diaz Ordaz ordered snipers to shoot the students. How tragic and ironic that Mexican leaders used U.S. weapons to kill students protesting for a more democratic government while agents from the Soviet Union encouraged the demonstrations.

Triggered by this knowledge and my memories of running across advancing troop lines on the *Avenida de la Reforma* in Mexico City, I created the fictional *On Wings of Silence: Mexico, 1968* with details supported by primary historical sources--testimonies from *Massacre in Mexico*, photos, letters, and newspapers, some with my byline.

Diana's friends and acquaintances are fictional, with one exception. The student leader with the white van was real and a total mystery. I suspect he was a U.S. government agent whose purpose was to destabilize student leadership in the American university during turbulent times.

And *Guillermo*? Like my protagonist, I grieve for him, for all of the *Guillermos* and *Guillerminas*, and their families. Their truncated lives and unrealized dreams will forever haunt me. Diana and I hope our voices will rise on the wings of their silence.

Half a century ago, Olympic posters read, *Todo es possible en la paz.* I share that belief, but now have the maturity to know that peace is only possible when we put away our weapons and listen to one another.

For More Information

Massacre in Mexico by Elena Poniatowska

1968: The Year that Rocked the World by Mark Kurlansky

http://www.npr.org/templates/story/story.php?storyId=97546687
http://nsarchive.gwu.edu/NSAEBB/NSAEBB10/intro.htm
http://www.cnn.com/WORLD/9802/04/mexico.massacre/
http://news.bbc.co.uk/onthisday/hi/dates/stories/october/2/newsid_3548000/354
8680.stm
http://www.nytimes.com/2007/07/11/world/americas/11students.html?_r=0
https://www.nytimes.com/2018/10/01/world/americas/mexico-tlatelolco-massacre.html
https://mexiconewsdaily.com/news/laques-honoring-president-are-coming-down/
http://www.latinorebels.com/2018/10/05/tlatelolcomassacrephotoessay/